NO MAN IS AN ISLAND

A Caleb Michael Smith Mystery

Andrew Harris Payne

ISBN: 1536891630
ISBN 13: 9781536891638
Library of Congress Control Number: 2016912936
CreateSpace Independent Publishing Platform
North Charleston, South Carolina

ACKNOWLEDGEMENTS

I would like thank the following people without whose support this book would not have been written:
Allan Rosner, Clint Corbett, and Becky Cole.

When Job's three friends, Eliphaz the Temanite, Bildad the Shuhite and Zophar the Naamathite, heard about all the troubles that had come upon him, they set out from their homes and met together by agreement to go and sympathize with him and comfort him.

Job 2:11

Thank you, also, to the group known informally as The Shelter Island Writers Group whose feedback and encouragement kept me going at this book.

Cover art by Matt Rohde. Please view more of his work at captain-kaos.smugmug.com

CHAPTER INTRO

Name: Caleb Michael Smith
Age: Adult
Occupation: Consultant/problem solver/reluctant assassin
Education: BA in history and Latin from Williams College, Williamstown, MA; PhD in electrical / bioengineering; PhD in mathematical physics, MIT. Unknown to any but his brother and father, Caleb has done research at the Institute for Advanced Study, Princeton, NJ, on the effect of human consciousness on elementary particles. His brother, Joshua, has a PhD in theology from the Catholic University of America and a PhD in mathematical topology from Princeton.
Religion: Roman Catholic, though he has played around with the idea of becoming an Eastern Catholic
Place of birth: North Island

There is evil in this world. It is very real, and it is usually very beautiful. It will smile at you coquettishly; it will caress your face; it will kiss you open-mouthed and whisper delicious sounds in your ear. You close your eyes and marinate in the juices of the seduction, and oh, it feels so good, so right. But before you realize what is happening, your throat is slit, and you are hanging upside down from a rusty hook, in the dark, bleeding through your neck and mouth and nose yet unable to die. You catch a glimpse of others around you, for there are many hanging, bleeding. Some are screaming through gurgling gushes of blood, and some merely writhe and twist in the unending agony of it all. Some hang motionless, resigned to their eternal fate, forever feeling life drain from them.

Be very careful, lest you find yourself hanging from a hook, in the dark, unable to die.

FROM THE DIARY OF CALEB MICHAEL SMITH

*R*ussia was a nightmare. I hate Russia. Well, not Russia, really, but what happens in Russia. There is much that is evil in Russia. When I was in Saint Petersburg, I needed God more than I have ever needed Him but still could not feel Him. Two Orthodox priests murdered. Flayed to the bone, hanging from ropes in front of the altar. Thank God that they were found before any of the congregants for Divine Liturgy saw them. There were no clues. But God gave me good friends. I sent what little information I collected to Harry in Boston. If anyone on Earth will be able to tell a story from some blood and a tooth, Harry Martin will.

I am angry. Father Konstantin Orlov was a good friend to me and Harry and Joshua. What am I going to do? I cannot let this go unavenged. Joshua is numb, but his faith is rock solid. He and Koni were classmates during Josh's time in Russia. I have been chasing this evil all over the world. Two priests, two good men butchered in their own church! If that is not evil, I do not know what is. I am going to kill the shit out of whoever did this. Koni had a wife and kids. I had to break the news to Anouchka. I am a grown man, so I remained stoic inside and out while this good and holy woman shook with grief in my arms. Telling her children was worse. I wish that my Russian were not so good. I understood everything those poor children said through their sobs. Please, God, keep their faith strong. Right *now I am mulling over my first steps. It is going to take a bit of planning, but this motherfucker is dead. I do not like killing, and I got into this business to solve one murder—the only one I have not figured out. One. How did it go this far? How many cases? Fifty? Sixty? I do not remember. All I know is that each seems more grisly than the last. My God, please give me just a little faith.*

(Added a few days later): *I found the piece of shit who killed my friends. I'm sure of it. I went to his apartment in Moscow, and he cowered in a corner like the bitch that he is. All over the walls were photographs of men and women he had abducted and butchered, including the priests. His kitchen looked like an abattoir. Even if I'm wrong about this scum killing the priests—and I'm not—this is a bad guy. So as he crouched in the corner begging for his life, I looked at a picture on his wall of a pretty girl with an "X" drawn in blood crossed over her face, and I put three bullets in that motherfucker's head. I know that he could not have acted alone, because there is no way that this pussy overpowered two priests, two men combat hardened in the Russian army, and then strung them up all by himself, but he had a hand in it. So I shot the piece of shit. Then I walked out of the apartment, down to the street, down to the corner and had coffee and a croissant in a café while talking to my brother on the phone.*

CHAPTER FIRST

C aleb Michael Smith was born in the year of our Lord nineteen hundred-something to the devout Catholic couple Arthur Payne Smith, known as Artie, and Mary Colvin Harris, on a rocky bump in the Atlantic called North Island.

He was born exactly one year to the day after his brother, Joshua. His brother, Joshua Payne Smith, had come before Cal almost as if in annunciation of the birth of his little brother.

When Caleb was born, his father and other relatives were present, in addition to the doctor and nurses. Artie's father was in the delivery room. Those cousins, uncles, aunts, and friends who could not be there in person sat by their phones waiting on pins and needles for news of the birth. It was a happy gathering, because Mary Smith had been told that after Joshua was born, she would be able to have no more children. This family was very close.

However, there was one in attendance, one who had also been awaiting this birth with great anticipation, who was not happy. A gray figure stood, unseen, in the birthing room. Only a deep sense of anxiety in Caleb's mother indicated something was not right.

Mary Smith told her obstetrician about how anxious she was, and the doctor chalked it up to hormones.

The gray figure was anxious as well, but she was anxious for this birth to turn out badly. That was this being's mission. If at all possible, the gray figure wanted this day to be the first and last day of the infant Caleb's life. Toward that end, this being of rot-ridden evil sent thoughts of hate and destruction at mother and yet-to-be-born child. She had slaughtered whole peoples in just such a way, and with far less effort. This timeless, immortal, yet ever-dying entity was suffused with a hate that would ensure this infant's death. So much rested on the obliteration of this tiny lump of flesh and the soul that inhabited it.

The gray figure focused a tight needle of hate. The lights above the doctor, nurses, and mother exploded in a cascade of sparks. Other lights simply went dark, and the figure smiled inwardly in satisfaction.

Something was wrong, though. There was still a light in the room. It was a light that had no Earthly source. Mary Smith's anxiety had led her to pray ever more fervently to God, and God had dispatched an unseen being of his own to act as lifelong guardian of Caleb Michael Smith, the Great Warrior Angel, the Archangel Micha-el.

A vision of Michael appeared to Mary Smith, and her anxiety was removed in an instant. At the same time, the vision appeared before the gray figure. Michael closed his wings about the gray figure, and a silent explosion of blinding light filled the room. The doctor dropped his instruments, the nurses fainted to the floor, and Artie Smith was knocked off his feet. When the light dissipated, Caleb Michael Smith was cradled in his mother's arms, clean and wrapped in a blanket on which, had they examined it carefully, they could have seen the faintest image of the face of the crucified Christ. That blanket would end up carefully folded in the infant's mother's hope chest, the image, to this day, unseen.

Caleb attended the local school with his brother and fifteen other students, graduating at the top of his class, as Joshua had done the previous year. Cal's childhood was idyllic, spent fishing, hunting, swimming, and reading books by James Fenimore Cooper at the ends of jetties thrust out into the sea. It, like so many other things in life, was nearly perfect, but not quite.

On a warm and beautiful, nearly perfect, late Spring day, Caleb and his brother were walking home from Caleb's last day of high school. Caleb was sixteen years old. Joshua was home from his first year at seminary. Cal and Josh were chatting about Josh's experiences at seminary when they saw a girl a little way ahead, also on her way home. She should have arrived home already but instead had stopped to crouch by the side of the road. She was talking to herself in what sounded to them like gibberish. She was also drawing odd symbols in the dirt with a stick. She was blond and beautiful, with skin that had a warm, soft, caramel glow throughout the year. Her name was Ora, meaning "light" in Hebrew. She had been created specifically for Caleb.

Cal had seen that light in her very early in his life and had been mesmerized by Ora from the first time he and she had played together as little children. That was the plan.

His thrall had been cemented on the day he saw her in a short, sheer sarong, covering, yet showing to great effect, a white-and-yellow bikini while she was walking past his family's house on her way home from the beach. Ora had no sense of shame, and even at the age of fifteen, she behaved with a casual disregard for social norms.

Ora's choice of bikini, her route past the Smith house, and anything else she did regarding Caleb were no accident. Ora knew that her beauty, from her hair color to her smile to the particular lilt of her voice, was something that Caleb found irresistible.

As the boys got closer, the girl's voice got clearer, and they could see the symbols she was drawing, but neither what she was saying nor the symbols made any sense to them. Cal and Josh stood there, watching her talk away to herself and draw nonsense in the dirt. Josh, not so enchanted as Cal—for he had special protection from such as Ora—said, "Ora, what are you doing?"

The girl, her beautiful honey-blond hair touching the ground as she crouched, continued to scribble and talk away in her gibberish and did not answer.

Josh spoke up again. "Ora, what are you doing?"

At that, Ora looked up from her doings on the ground. "Hello, boys," she said, smiling. The girl stood, turned, and as she did, stared directly at Caleb with her piercing green-blue eyes. Cal felt the look in his gut. Then she turned her back on them, crouched, and went back to her babbling and scratching and would not be roused from them.

Josh looked over to Cal and whispered, as if the girl before them could not hear, "This is what you're so hot for?"

On hearing Josh, the girl smiled to herself. She liked knowing that Cal was hot for her, for she knew that she had been created specifically for Caleb.

Cal knew where Joshua was going with this line of talk. He'd heard it all before.

Josh continued, "I may be in seminary, but I'm still a man, and I see how hot she is. And even though I'm not supposed to judge her, lemme tell ya, she's a fuckin' weirdo. And she always smells as if she's just thrown up."

Cal looked at Josh and said, "But look at her! Besides, she does not smell like that. To me, she sometimes smells like suntan lotion or freshly cut pine or even warm cookies just out of the oven. But not vomit."

Josh raised a disapproving eyebrow at Cal. "I've got eyes and a dick, but no fuckin' way, Cal. No fuckin' way."

The two moved on, leaving the blond beauty to whatever it was she was doing.

As they walked away, Cal said to Josh, "You know, Josh, you swear an awful lot for a guy studying to be a priest."

Josh smiled and said, "Fuckin' A, Cal."

The boys walked on. At what Cal considered a safe distance, he could not resist looking back over his shoulder for one more glance at the crazy and mysteriously weird girl to whom he was so attracted. She had risen to her feet, her blond hair blowing about her head, and had turned in the direction that the boys were walking. Cal could see that her face was calm and smiling at him as if she knew that he would look back at her. The beautiful girl looked almost like she might run after them, but she stayed right where she was. She waved at Cal, turned, and crouched again. The boys walked on, talking and laughing with each other. Soon they were out of sight of Ora.

Ora continued with her scratching and babbling but in a few minutes fell from her crouch to the ground, unconscious. Her face went from young to old to nothing at all, in a sickening montage of diabolic roiling chaos. Then her normal girl's face found itself; she awoke and stood, instinctively looking in the direction of where the boys had walked, but remembered none of what had happened in the preceding hour. These lapses were happening with increasing frequency, and they upset her. She had spoken to her father, a physician by training, and he had told her that it was normal for a girl, sometimes, to have these things happen around her time of the month. It was about to be that time now, so maybe he was right.

Ora knew that her father carried some dark secret. She knew something cold lived inside him, though she did not know what that might be. She was afraid of that thing coming alive in her, yet, she almost welcomed it. So confusing!

When Ora had asked her mother about the spells, her mother had gotten a frightened look on her face and said that her father was right. When Ora went back to her father again about the "spells," he got that look in his eyes, and she knew not to bring it up again.

As the boys walked, Cal felt cold even on this warm day and grabbed Joshua's arm. "Come on, Joshua, I want to stop by Fitz's swimming hole. There have got to be a bunch of kids down there by now, and this is my last year to be a kid."

"Caleb, you've never been a kid. But OK, let's go."

The brothers' ten-minute walk took them about thirty minutes; Josh just wanted to stop and look at every flower and bird they encountered.

The smell of hot dogs and hamburgers cooked over a makeshift barbecue met their noses as they approached the swimming hole. Cal and Josh heard the joyous laughter of children swimming and the raucous shouts of "Look out below!" from kids swinging from the tire on a rope.

Above the din, the boys could hear the shouts and laughing of their baby sister, Patty. She was the happiest, most carefree girl either of the brothers had ever known, and she liked to share her happiness with any boy within arm's reach. This worked out fine, because the entire island's population of some two thousand had had a very casual approach to sex for generations.

Who slept with whom and how often, and even the marital status of the parties involved, did not seem to matter much to anyone. Folks did pair off in what were, most of the time, lifelong partnerships, but if someone was lonely or having a bad spell, comfort was always just a phone call or an e-mail away, and no one thought anything of it.

Gathering at the swimming hole after the last day of school had been a tradition for a least a century and a half. Cal was also happy to be around the joy and lightheartedness, the kids playing and laughing. He had been having sad and troubling thoughts for about six months. He would sink into periods of deep melancholy for no reason, at least no reason he could figure out. Caleb had told no one of these episodes, not even Josh, and he told Josh just about everything.

"Hey, look, it's Josh and Caleb!" yelled Ora's older sister, a softly curvaceous and extremely beautiful girl named Gemma, as her head emerged from the water. Gemma could have easily partaken of the island's laissez-faire attitude toward sex, but for Gemma Dufaigh there was one man only: Caleb Michael Alexander Smith.

In a shot, most of the swimmers had come out of the water to greet their old friends. Josh and Cal were very popular, and having Josh back on the island was like having a celebrity in their midst. The kids slapped Josh on the back, all asking questions at the same time. Most of the girls were of the opinion that Joshua Smith being a priest was a waste of a perfectly sexy man. Some of them did not know that they would be granted their wish, Josh's vocation notwithstanding.

Josh did his best to answer the questions thrown at him. It was the custom for both boys and girls to swim in their skivvies, a nod to the easy attitude toward sex and nudity that pervaded the island population. Josh looked wide-eyed at the girls in only their underwear, and he, too, began to question his vocation for just a moment.

Cal saw the look in his brother's eyes and said, deep-voiced but in a joking way, "Father Josh! Eyes to yourself!"

Then, close to Josh's ear, Caleb said, "Never gets old, does it?" and he gave his older brother an elbow to the ribs.

"No, it does not. Priest or not, I don't know if I can ever give it up."

Gemma did not join in the fracas. She stayed in the water, floating on her back, picturing Caleb naked and smiling privately.

She was in love with Caleb but let no one else know it, other than her mother. She thought of herself and Cal alone on a beach, making out on a towel while the briny air played with her long dark hair.

Cal stepped away from his brother as the other kids crowded around Josh. He felt a warmth come from inside himself. He had been with almost every girl here, and the thought made him happy.

When he felt this warmth, he became aroused, and it could happen at any time and place, such as here and now when he was about to strip down to his underwear.

No matter, he thought. *This won't be the first time girls have seen the gallant response from me, or from any of the other boys here.*

He walked a few steps toward the water and saw Gemma floating there with her head toward him so that he was looking at her from her head to her feet. He was sure that she could not see him. Her eyes looked closed.

However, as he watched her floating, she raised her arm, turned her hand with its long, feminine fingers, and did a little wave at him. Cal was amazed and wondered how she did that. The thought of telepathy crossed his mind. But Caleb was a very serious young man, not given to things spiritual or even conventionally religious.

For her part, Gemma felt the warmth return from Caleb, and it gave her tingles. Gemma even knew that Caleb had the hots for Ora. This did not really bother her. Gemma also knew that he loved her but that the time was not right. The time would not be right for a long while. She could wait. She could wait for a thousand years for something she knew was coming.

One boy, a very good friend of the Smiths, began to yell, "Throw him in, throw him in." In seconds, the whole throng was chanting. Before Josh realized what was happening, he was being picked up by a dozen boys and girls and was quite unceremoniously tossed into the swimming hole.

Caleb stood on the edge of the hole, laughing at his big brother until Gemma started to shout, "Caleb, too! Caleb, too!" Cal got a deer-in-the-headlights look and tried to run, but it was too late. Cal was tackled and thrown in next to his brother.

The brothers swam to a ledge where the water was about knee-deep, pulled themselves onto it, and bowed deeply to the crowd, who erupted in cheers and jumped into the water.

The boys got out of the water, stripped to their underwear, and hung their clothes on a tree branch to dry. They cannonballed themselves back into the water.

Cal got out and grabbed the tire swing, yelling, "Geronimo!" and flew high into the air, coming down with a great splash. When his head emerged from the water, he saw Ora standing on the edge the swimming hole, stripped down and smiling as if she had not seen them in the last forty-five minutes. A boy came up behind her, scooped her up in his arms, and jumped into the water next to Caleb, Ora squealing with delight the whole time.

Caleb floated in the water, waiting for the boy and Ora to bob to the surface. The boy was Harry Martin. He was a nice kid and best friend of Caleb and Joshua. In fact, he was considered by the Smiths and himself to be the third Smith brother.

Harry had not jumped into the water with Ora accidentally. No, Harry had been chosen by a larger reality, specifically because he and Caleb had been friendly rivals for Ora's affections for some time. Though Ora's native beauty was attractive to all the boys, it seemed that Harry was an unwitting suitor. He had been manipulated by powers far beyond his understanding to long for and chase after Ora. That was the idea. It was not the truth, but it was the idea.

North Island was a strange and special place. Most of the people living on it were strange and special, too. One of North Island's most strangely special people was Harry Martin. So Harry Martin, thought by Angels dark and devious to be like a puppet on strings, was no such thing at all. He was one of them, though these dark Angels did not know that. Harry, long before his birth, had flipped sides and was now working for the Light.

When the pair appeared, Ora looked at Caleb for just a second, turned to Harry, and kissed him square on the mouth. Caleb felt the jealousy that Ora had intended, but he suppressed it so that Ora would not see how he felt.

Harry broke the kiss and swam over to Caleb. He said to Caleb in a low voice and with a wink, "Don't worry, old man. You know how I like to poke around in things that are already dead. Besides, there's Janie, just sitting on the ledge behind you. You know she's wet for you. Go have some fun and forget about blond corpses. They're my thing."

Caleb did not know what Harry, a boy as close to him as his own brother, meant by that remark—and why did Harry always call him "old man"? He knew that Harry was obsessed with all things dead and wanted to be a forensic pathologist, but how did that apply to Ora?

Harry always acted as if he knew more about Caleb than he let on, and sometimes this made Caleb uneasy around his friend.

What slept inside Caleb were worlds of power, worlds of knowledge, worlds of understanding so vast that, had he been made fully aware of them at this age, they would have instantly killed him.

Harry knew what was inside Caleb, waiting for its time to awaken, but told Caleb nothing. Still, Cal felt confused by everything lately: his spells of sadness; Ora's strangeness; Gemma's odd, if pleasant, behavior; and Harry. He decided to put it out of his mind and took Harry's advice. He turned and dived beneath the surface of the water, came out on the other side of the swimming hole, and sat on a rock ledge next to the pretty brunette. Jane already had a crush on Caleb, so she did not mind his attention at all.

It was now Ora's turn to hide her feelings. A dark hatred filled her, and she could feel stirrings of things old and familiar within herself, like the smell of rotting flesh, like watching something die for the fun of it. These stirrings roused within her a sort of pleasure that threw her. These odd movings from within were becoming more frequent, and though they frightened and confused her a little, the feelings did not scare her so much that she wanted them to stop.

Ora looked over to Caleb, who was by now kissing Jane, and said to Harry, "C'mon, let's get out of here." She tugged Harry by the arm, and the two swam to the edge of the hole. Harry pulled himself up and out of the water and then lent a hand to Ora. He looked over to Cal with a questioning face. Cal looked back at Harry and gave him the high sign, which meant that everything was good and the friendship between them solid.

Fifteen-year-old Patty Smith, natural empath, the baby of the Smith family, was dangling her legs at the edge of the water. She had watched the whole scene from when her brothers had arrived to the point when Caleb started kissing Jane.

She had seen Gemma wave at Caleb, and with it, Caleb's astonishment. She had seen Gemma's sister, Ora, do whatever it was that Ora did, and she had felt Caleb's jealousy, even though he had hidden it well. She felt the strength of Joshua as he let the raw sexual energy of the girls who were hot for him wash through and over him while not allowing it to move him an inch. She thought that he was making the wrong decision in pursuing his vocation, because she had sexual energy washing over and through her every day, and it always moved her. Just about every boy here had kissed Patty at one time or another. She hoped that Josh would not take final vows.

Patty had watched all of this with a detached and almost amused air, feeling it all, understanding most of it. She looked over at Gemma, whom she loved dearly, the big sister born to another mother, who was now sitting directly across the swimming hole from her. Patty marveled at Gemma's composure as she watched Caleb kiss another girl. Patty would have been wild with jealousy in Gemma's place. Then she felt Gemma's faith and strength and understood that, too.

After another couple of hours of swimming, tire swinging, and barbecuing, kids were beginning to leave. Tonight would be the big bonfire and another barbecue at Cornelius Beach, and nobody wanted to miss it.

Josh had been swimming and talking with old friends. One boy, whose name was Jonathan, was thinking about the seminary. He was the one who had yelled to throw Josh in the water. Jonathan, because of his call to the priesthood, had deliberately called for Josh's dunking to spare Josh any further temptation from the half-dressed girls, girls who tempted Jonathan, himself. Josh looked at his diver's watch and realized that it was time to go. He broke off his conversation with Jonathan, promising to talk to him that night. He found Caleb, who was now high in the tree from which the tire swing was suspended, getting ready for one last cannonball.

"Come on, Cal. If we're going to have time to help Pops with some chores and get ready for the bonfire, we need to leave now!"

"OK, Josh! Here I come!" Cal jumped from a height of some fifteen feet and came down with a giant splash. He sank beneath the surface. Cal opened his eyes while under the water. He remembered the old island story of a girl being lured to the swimming hole by an old woman, only to have her throat slit in sacrifice to an evil deity. Her blood was drained into the water, and she was finally thrown, decapitated, into the depths of the spring. With that, Cal saw a Halloween witch's hag face in front of him. She reached out with two gnarled hands and held him under. As her hands touched his skin, images, hundreds of them, flashed through his mind's eye: the girl of the story, feeling the horror of the life draining from her body; small boys, grown men and women, hanging upside down, dripping blood into this very water from throats ripped open by the claws of a woman animal of unimaginable ferocity; drooling evil, living on the island through millennia. These images and others gripped Cal with the hands of the hag. He started to take water into his lungs and was sure that he was going to drown. Then she was gone. Cal popped to the surface, gasping. He looked at Josh, who said with a smile, "Let's go, old boy!"

Caleb asked, "How long was I under?"

Josh said, "I don't know, a few seconds, maybe?" To Cal, it had felt like five minutes. Cal was shaken, but he decided to drop it— too much weird stuff today.

They retrieved their clothes, got dressed, and made their way home, with Caleb talking about their plans for the Summer the whole way to take his mind off what he'd just experienced under the water of the swimming hole.

When the boys got home, their mother met them at the front door. Mary Colvin Harris Smith was in her late forties but looked to be in her early thirties. With long dark hair and a warm smile, Mrs. Smith was like a sexy Betty Crocker with a high IQ. Today, though, she was not smiling.

"Mom, what's the matter? Why are you crying?" Caleb asked. Joshua put his arm around his mother, leading her into their living room, and sat down next to her.

"Caleb, Joshua, I don't know how to say this…" She trailed off, weeping into her hands.

Cal sat down on the other side of his mother and also put his arm around her, thinking the worst. "Is Pop OK? Has anything happened to Pop?"

At the thought of losing her beloved husband, Mary Smith wept all the more and said through tears, "No, good Lord have mercy, no. The Jorgensen boy was killed today after school. He was only ten. His mother told me that he was found lying on Driven Beach about thirty minutes ago. There were marks on his neck, as if he'd been strangled. There were symbols scratched into his stomach, too. The police don't know what to make of any of it yet. Dear God in heaven, his mother is absolutely numb. The ferries and airstrip have been shut down so no one can get off the island. I'm going over to see her now, but I wanted to tell you before I left. What am

I going to say to her? If I ever lost one of you boys, I'm not sure I would be able to…"

She could not finish her sentence. Mrs. Mary Colvin Harris Smith, her face streaming with tears, hugged her boys close to her. Cal and Josh sat on the sofa, dumbstruck, not knowing what to say. Cal, especially, was angry. The news of Asgeir's death touched that melancholic place Cal had visited too often lately. He did not know why, but he felt that maybe the dark place and the death of the boy were connected, that the sadness was a message that he could not decipher.

They sat there for a few minutes, Cal using the time to regain his composure. They were stirred from their torpor by the phone.

Josh stood to answer it, but Mary said, "No, Joshua, let me."

Mary dried her eyes, picked up the old black Bakelite receiver, put it to her ear, and said faintly, "Hello?"

Cal and Josh could hear the muffled sobs coming from the phone, and Mary said, "Oh, Sue, I'm coming right over. Please, I'm sorry—I just had to tell my boys." She looked at them and started to cry all over again.

Sue Jorgensen was an Icelandic transplant to North Island. A woman of about the same age as Mary, also beautiful but blond, she had had Asgeir (meaning "spear of the gods" in Old Norse) after being told that she would never have children. She was then thirty-nine and could hear her clock ticking loudly, and Asgeir had been the blessing of all blessings.

From the beginning he had been a sweet child, sleeping through the night and crying only seldom. As he grew, he was a light to all who knew him, often behaving much older than his years. He spoke out loud to beings he called "his Angels" and could describe their appearance in detail.

He had shown a way with the elderly that had astounded people, talking to them and empathizing with them, so his parents, at his request, began taking him to the aged and infirm.

Many were the times he would walk over to elderly men or women in their last days, looking hopeless and alone, put a hand on their shoulder, and whisper in their ear, only to have a smile of peace and contentment come over the old one's face. Asgeir would never tell anyone what he said, nor would his elderly friends.

When asked what the boy had whispered to him, a man who was just over a hundred said, "Son, if you're lucky enough, one day you may find out." He then closed his eyes and passed happily.

Now that light had been snuffed out. In that moment, Cal knew. He knew what he was going to do with his life. He was going to find out what had killed Asgeir Jorgensen.

CHAPTER CALEB

O n the west wall of his house was the stereo system purchased by his grandfather and manufactured by a company named McIntosh in an era long before the geeks in
Cupertino had stopped wetting their beds. The equipment had
tubes that lit up with a fiery red glow and gave off a warmth
that always made Cal nostalgic for a time that had all but ended before he was even conceived. This marvelous example of
mid-twentieth-century high technology was flanked on both
sides by banks of real, honest-to-goodness, 33 1/3 rpm LPs sitting in mahogany racks fashioned by Caleb's own hand.

On the uppermost rack were Duke Ellington and Art Tatum
records. Just below were the Allman Brothers Band and Jean-Luc
Ponty, and on the lowest rack, just about at waist level, were the
Beatles albums, the first of which, *Beatles for Sale*, was given to
Caleb by his brother.

Caleb's record collection was a reflection, not only of his musical tastes, but of who was inside of himself. Caleb was a man of

few words. He preferred to let his work—and when needed, his fists—do his talking.

On his wrist he wore a very expensive, self-winding Swiss watch with a black dial and no numerals. On his face, titanium-framed eyeglasses, black to match his watch, partially hid piercing blue-green eyes.

This night, he had just returned from a "business trip" abroad. He wore black cashmere trousers and a dark-gray button-down shirt with a matching knit tie. His feet sported American-made black leather penny loafers with Mercury dimes, minted in the year of his father's birth, inserted in each tongue. When Caleb traveled he did not feel comfortable unless he was properly dressed—proper yet not stuffy.

A pistol lay on the shelf next to his turntable. It was a custom-built .45 caliber. He favored .45s because of the round's tremendous stopping power. Cal did not like the gun, but it had saved his life on several occasions.

It was late evening, and Caleb was tired. Flying always drained him. As he stood in front of the German-made turntable, he appreciated that it was crafted with all the precision that Caleb demanded of his things.

His strong, masculine hands at the ends of tanned, muscular arms held his newly purchased LP pressing of *The Beatles*, popularly known as *The White Album*.

He carefully removed the pristine vinyl disc from the cover and inner sleeve, quietly taking in that beautiful new-record chemical smell.

He loved LP records because vinyl LPs had become almost as rare as rotary phones, which he also owned. The man used digital photography because it served his work, and he was a computer programmer, but he had decided years before that he would never brook digital music in any of its ghastly forms.

So there he stood, balancing the record between his middle finger and the meaty part of his square hand, thinking, almost off dreaming, silently sifting through the data in his head and the emotions in his heart.

He placed the disc over the spindle on the platter and carefully cleaned its grooves. He moved the tone arm over to the lead-in for the first track and lowered the stylus. The beautiful, empty quiet of diamond needle on black vinyl played through the speakers; the reassuring ticks and pops were just audible from the cool, dark surface of the record. The jet engines of "Back in the USSR" began to soar into the room, rattling some glassware on either side of the speakers.

The sounds were old and familiar and soothed his tired brain. Cal had been listening to this record since he was a small boy, and he loved the sound of it.

He walked over to his sofa, sitting down in the space left him by his two dogs, and listened to the tight, well-rehearsed band. The Fab Four had toyed with the idea of breaking up, and had even taken a two-year hiatus from releasing any music. During that two-year period, they had been very hard at work in the studio, changing their musical direction and, once again, changing music history forever. Caleb was very glad that they had decided against breaking up.

His phone rang, jolting him out of his musical trance. Cal looked at the name of the caller. He knew the man well, as well as he knew his own father. "Hello, Jonas. I had hoped I would not hear from you."

After a moment, Cal said, "I know. I know. After what I went through in Russia, I knew that the time was soon. I had hoped I was wrong."

Cal listened to the old man's reply. "I understand." He switched off his phone. He did not want any more calls that night.

He again drifted off into a reverie, as he always seemed to do when recovering from a case—whenever he had a free two minutes, even—thinking of this and that and nothing at all.

"You don't know how lucky you are, boy, back in the US, back in the US, back in the USSR…" came from the speakers, bringing him back to himself.

Cal had just finished a job in Saint Petersburg. It had been the worst of his career: two dead priests, gruesomely murdered by what turned out to be an itinerant madman. Caleb was very glad to be out of Russia.

It was already getting toward daybreak, and as he listened, his exhausted eyelids began to close. He reached for the rosary brought to him from the Vatican by one of his best friends. In the Rosary, Caleb had always tried to find strength and peace. He would need some measure of strength, for he was not alone in the room.

As Caleb got closer and closer to the sleep he so badly wanted, his left hand relaxed, and the rosary fell to the floor. Just before he finally drifted off to sleep, he heard the softly dreamy, chillingly seductive voice of someone he thought had been gone forever, calling his name—the gray figure present at his birth.

"Caleb Smith? Caleb?"

Cal stirred on the couch, and the two dogs growled in the low tones that dogs have when they sense danger.

A gray hand waved itself over the dogs, and they fell silent. "Tonight is your lucky night, filthy mongrels." Then the voice said, in Russian, "*Dirty scum.* "Snuffing you now would be too easy. It would give me away too soon. You get to live your wretched lives for another day, so shut up now."

The rotting gray hand reached down to the floor and picked up the beads Caleb had dropped earlier. The other hand moved to Caleb's face and caressed it almost lovingly. A wave of nostalgia from experiences had over many centuries swept over the gray form standing beside the sofa. This feeling was instantly replaced with a homicidal anger. The hand was quickly withdrawn.

"I ought to kill you for that, dear Caleb. Those days were long ago and far away."

The form's empty eyes soaked in Caleb's visage, while dark bile dripped slowly from toothless gaps in its jaw and onto the floor. Festering lesions oozed pus from the creature's cheeks and lips. Great empty spaces showed where flesh once was.

The gray hand returned to Cal's face, and the creature spoke in a soft, soothing voice these words: "Caleb Michael Smith. Cal. Caleb. Caleb Michael Smith. What I am going to do to you would make the worst in history cringe."

Then, with a sigh, it continued in gentle but deeper, more powerful tones. "I am going to kill your dogs. I am going to kill your parents and your brother and sister. I am going to kill that fat cow, Gemma.

"Today is not your day, either, dead man. However, when your hour comes, then, oh then, Cal, I am going to slowly drain the life out of you. I am going to suffocate your soul. You will die in such pain that you will beg for death. I will not give you death, not right away, but you will die, my old friend Caleb."

A loud boom echoed throughout the house, and every window in the little place imploded, scattering shards in all directions, and the creature was gone.

He slept on the large Mission-style sofa, a dog in back of him, a dog in front of him. He slept in fits and starts. The dogs had been restless all afternoon, as well.

Dark dreams clouded and racked his slumber, and he awoke before sunset to the sound of a boom and the hiss of a million scalpels of glass flying from the window frames into the house. Missy and Jacob, long-hair and wire-hair miniature dachshunds, respectively, began to bark loudly and were yelping as if in pain.

He lay there, staring into the room, stunned, still trying to get his bearings. His ears were ringing. His head was pounding. Small bits of window were standing at attention on the exposed skin of his arms, legs, and face.

Caleb put a hand out in the dark and felt for Jacob's head. Jake let out a yelp, and he knew that his dogs were hurt, too.

Caleb called out, feeling the sting from dozens of cuts on his face, "Lights on, one hundred percent."

The lights illuminated sheer destruction. He was foggy and disoriented from the dream of the crazy gray woman. He wondered if he was still dreaming. Then he looked straight up and saw it: a cross, drawn upside down from his point of view, drawn in what looked like ash from a fireplace. He steeled himself to take action. This would not go unanswered.

Caleb carefully put his hands around Jacob, brought the little dog to his chest, and slowly sat up. The sharp sting of literally a thousand cuts made him wince, and little Jacob cried out in his own pain. Missy had been curled up in a tight ball when the glass flew and was at least spared shards in her nose and near her eyes. Cal reached for his phone, which lay on the end table behind his head.

He spoke into the phone: "Call Patty." The phone responded in Gemma's voice: "Calling Patty." In his parents' house, his sister saw her phone move across the kitchen table as it vibrated.

Cal had, as a joke to annoy his baby sister, programmed her phone to ring with the phrase "Patty, youah wicked cute!" and had "fixed" the phone so that Patty could not fix it herself. He refused to put it back the way it was, because it annoyed her so. She caught the phone just as it was going to fall off the table.

"Caleb, when the hell are you going to put my phone back to the normal ringtone?"

Cal spoke in a normal voice. "Patty, I need you to come over."

"What's the matter, Cal?"

"Nothing big. Just come over, OK?"

Patty put her phone in her jeans pocket, walked into the living room, craned her neck around a corner, and called up to her parents, "Mom, Dad! I'm going to see Cal."

Artie and Mary Smith had gone upstairs late in the afternoon this day to, in the words of Artie, "do their stamp collecting." The couple had been very dedicated to stamps lately.

These two have got to have the best stamp collection in the continental United States by now, she thought. *Come to think of it, I need my postage canceled, too.*

Her father yelled down from his place next to his wife. "Why are you going to see Cal?"

"He called me and asked me to come over."

"Is anything wrong?"

"No. He just wants me to mind the dogs while he goes out. You know how he is," she lied.

Artie Smith rolled onto his side, pulled his wife's back close to him, and said, "When is that girl going to learn that I know when she's lying even before she opens her mouth?"

"She's just trying to protect you or cover for her brother. You know that," his wife replied through giggles.

"I do know that she's a good girl. She's been a good girl to a lot of men on this island. She also has a good heart. She was made that way. No matter how wild our child is, I know that she's good underneath it all."

Patty was in her car by then, racing toward her brother's house. She was filled with anxiety, mostly because Cal was not answering his phone.

Cal had negotiated his way through broken glass to the bathroom. The sight of his face in the mirror was frightening; his face was cut in dozens of places. *There is not enough toilet paper on North Island to stop this bleeding,* he thought somberly. He tweezed the glass splinters and stood there, watching himself bleed.

Cal washed and dried his face, put a couple of small bandages on the larger cuts, and went back to the sofa to continue to pick points of glass out of his dogs, who steadfastly endured this torture.

Patty ran up to his door and burst through. What she saw stopped her cold. The inside of the house was strewn with shards of glass. She looked to her left to see her brother holding Jacob's snout in his hands as he pulled glass from the little dog's nose.

"What the hell happened?"

"I don't know. I feel that something doesn't want me to probe any deeper into things. I was asleep, really deeply asleep but having bad dreams, dreams of a being who is like a walking corpse. This same dream haunted my nights in Saint Petersburg. These dreams have haunted me since I was a boy."

"I remember," said Patty.

"I thought I was rid of the dreams. I was, for a long while."

"I had hoped that you were rid of them."

"Well, I can't remember most of it, but it felt so real, like she was here in the room. Then the glass exploded, just the way you see it. I'm still a little dazed."

"I'm sure you are. What can I do?"

Cal, lost in his own thoughts, replied, "I've been chasing evil all over the world for ten years. Now it's chasing me."

Patty looked at her brother with bewilderment and concern in her eyes. "OK, well, this is no time to figure it out. Let's start cleaning up."

Cal stood up, again picked his way through the glass, and handed the tweezers to Patty. "Take this; tend to the dogs. Jacob is worse off than Missy. I've got to get dressed and get these windows boarded up. Damn, first I need to clean up the glass, at least the bigger shards."

He went to his bedroom and changed his clothes, making sure to put on his heaviest work boots. He went outside, grabbed a flat shovel and his shop vac from his workshop, and went back to the house to start the cleanup.

After the glass was mostly cleared away, Cal said, "I want you and the dogs to come with me, Patty. Got to take care of some business."

"Where are we going?"

"I've got some work to do for some cases, and I do not want you and the pups here alone. Also, I don't want to leave them in the car alone, so I want you to take them back to Mom and Pop's place to look after them. I will bring back all the rocky-road ice cream you can eat. Deal?"

"Deal," said Patty.

Dogs tended to and vet appointments made, windows and doors boarded over, Cal, Patty, and the dogs made their way outside and breathed in the cold November air. The frigid wind stung the cuts on Cal's face and hands. Still, it was good to be outside. The cold air focused his mind.

Cal thought he knew what had been behind the events of the day. He felt—somewhere very deep in a place that gave him vertigo to look at—that he had been fighting the gray demon forever and ever and ever. Fatigue welled up from that place, so Caleb hardened himself against the fatigue; he beat the tiredness into a submission that would last for many hours.

The screeching of an eagle came diving out of the sky, and Caleb looked up but could not see it. He heard it again directly above him and still saw nothing. He did, however, feel better. He found that iron place within and set his jaw. A new energy took hold of him, and he leaped off the porch, skipping four steps, and ran for his Jeep, with Patty, carrying Jacob and Missy beating everyone else to the car on her short, but very nimble legs.

When he and Patty and the pups were sitting in the car with the engine warming up, he felt a presence beside him. That is when he remembered his friend Father Konstantin Orlov and that *Orlov* means "eagle" in Russian.

Cal looked up. "Koni, you Russian bastard, was that you?" He put the car in gear, drove to his parents' house, and walked Patty and the dogs inside.

His father and mother took one look at him and the dogs, and his father asked, "Good Lord, son. What happened to you?"

Cal replied, "Pops, before I go, I want to talk to you about something."

"What is it, Cal?" his mother asked.

"Something between Pops and me, Mom. Please try to understand."

"I do, sweetheart, I do. There are some things that men just have to keep 'men things.' You two go and talk. Patty and I will make sure the dogs are all right."

Caleb and his father walked into the backyard and sat down at a picnic table across from each other.

"I have a feeling I know what this is about, son," Caleb's father said.

"I bet you do, Dad."

"'Dad' is it now? You *are* upset. You call me 'Dad' only when you're really 'round the bend."

"You're goddamned right I'm upset! I hate this ridiculous Bible-faith-angel mumbo jumbo."

"Now, son, I know how this sort of thing sticks in your craw, but this is who we are. You're just going to have to accept it for now, hold your nose, and do what you're supposed to do according to prophecy."

"Another word I hate. Whose prophecy, anyway?"

"God's."

"'God's,' he says! I pray and pray and pray, and it feels like I'm pissing up a rope for all the good it does."

"And still you pray."

"Yes."

"Why is that, do you suppose?"

"Because you and Mom and Gemma say that I ought to."

"Cal, you're a grown man. You don't do *anything* that you don't want to do. Never have. Not even when you were a child. So why do you pray?"

"This conversation is taking a wrong turn, Pops. I brought you out here to talk about Jonas."

"I know, my boy. Believe it or not, we are talking about Jonas."

"How's that?"

"Because Jonas Smith is a praying man and your grandfather's brother, my own uncle. He's as close to you as any man alive, and he must have called you last night, or you wouldn't be here. He would not have called you if he had not been *praying* and got a sign that now was the time."

"I don't want to do it, Dad."

"I know, son, but you must. You've done much worse in your profession, haven't you?"

"That's different, Pops. Those guys deserved what they got."

"Well, think of it that way, then. Jonas deserves this, too. Not because he's a bad man, but because he's a good man, a good and faithful servant of the Lord, and this is his reward."

"Why isn't he scared?" asked Caleb.

"Because when he was your age, longer ago than you think, he got the same call, though it wasn't a phone call, and he's been waiting for this his entire life."

"What? That means that someday…" Caleb trailed off, everything becoming clear and his stoicism and sense of duty returning.

"Yes, son, I see that you understand. You always did. You simply did not want to acknowledge it."

"Yes, Pops. I have to go."

"Go with my blessing *and* Jonas's blessing, too."

Cal and Arthur stood up from the picnic table. Cal hugged his father and left without going back in the house.

As Cal's hand touched his car door, he spun around, went back to his parent's front door, opened it and yelled for his doggy buddies to come with him.

The dogs came running with Patty not far behind them. "I thought you wanted Jacob and Missy with me?"

"I do", said Caleb, "but I want them with me for just a little longer. I need them. I will bring them back very soon."

Cal turned and left without further explanation. He did not want explain to the women where he was going, because they were not to be privy to this part of his life.

CHAPTER NEXT

Cal hoisted himself and the dogs up into the Jeep, depressed the clutch, shifted to first, and started slowly down the tree-lined lane away from his parents' house.

His route took him to a road that did not have a formal name, but everyone on North Island called it the Perimeter Road. He could have gone a more direct route and gotten to his destination in five minutes. However, he wanted to think this through. Not think, really, but feel, which he did not like doing. He needed to feel this through so that when he came to the house where he wanted to be, he would be ready.

In about twenty-five minutes of slow, careful driving, Cal came upon the island's western lighthouse, known by islanders as West Light. He pulled up to the keeper's quarters, let the dogs out to play and went in without knocking. There in the foyer of the little cedar house stood a wizened old man wearing a Greek sailor's cap with a briarwood pipe sticking out of his mouth, he looked like a painting hanging in a gallery.

Cal stared directly into the old man's eyes and said, "It's time, isn't it?"

The old man nodded and said, "Come this way, and don't look so glum, my boy."

The old man led Caleb through the house to the kitchen, which smelled of venison stew and spiced wine. This kitchen had seen much love and merriment. It had also served as the birthing room of many of Caleb's relatives. It was a magical place.

The two men went out the back door, down ancient and crumbling stone steps, and across the back lawn of the property. Not one more word was spoken as they made their way to the cliffs that rose above the roiling waves some 250 feet below.

When they reached the edge, the older man turned to Caleb. A small tear hung in the corner of his eye.

Caleb asked, "Why do I have to do this, Jonas?"

"Because you do."

"I've killed men before. I don't want to do this."

"I know. Your father called to tell me that you were on your way. He explained as much to you as he could. You have to know that you are doing me a favor. I do not want to spend another five hundred years waiting around for the right Smith to be born so that I can go home. I'm too tired for that."

"Five hundred years?" Caleb was incredulous. "I don't believe it."

"I didn't ask you to believe it. You will someday see for yourself, and that's all I am going to say on the matter. Send me home now. Fulfill the prophecy. Please."

Caleb got very close to him and hugged the old man tight. The keeper hugged him in return. The embrace broke off, and the keeper stepped back just a few inches. He nodded to Caleb, and Caleb pushed the old man off the cliff with all of his strength. Cal stepped right to the edge and watched as the old lighthouse keeper was dashed on the rocks below.

"Jacob, Missy let's go," Caleb shouted.

He walked around the little house, looked up at the brick tower, and remembered all the times that he, Joshua, and their father had spent here talking with the old lighthouse keeper.

Cal and Josh were rarely privy to those conversations, but when the boys were allowed to sit at the kitchen table while the men drank coffee, often fortified with Irish whiskey, it was so that the boys could listen carefully.

To Joshua and Caleb, what the men said to them and to each other always felt familiar, as if they had heard it all before in some misty past, so long ago that even the rocks had forgotten.

On one visit, the men were inside, and the boys were outside throwing a football back and forth. Josh threw a hard spiral to Cal, and while the ball was in midthrow, Cal felt his father call him. Cal, distracted, let the ball hit him in his right eye, giving him a real shiner.

"You felt that, didn't you?" Josh said, laughing.

"You're darn right I felt that. It hit me right in the eye!"

"Not the football," Josh said. "You heard Dad calling you. I know you did, because I heard it, too."

"I did not hear it. I felt it," Caleb said, holding his hand up to his eye.

"Soon enough, you'll hear it, too. OK, let's go inside."

Cal snapped out of his daydream and got into his car with the dogs none-the-wiser for the events of the last half hour. He reached his parents' home, and after hugging his mother and sister, he went in to see his father. He called—with his thought only—to his father, who responded that he was in the den.

When Cal reached the den, he said, "It's done."

"I know, son. Jonas told me already."

"He told you? Look, Pops, I have never really gotten used to the idea that you and I and Josh can hear one another's thoughts. I don't want to hear about dead old men talking to you from beyond the grave."

"OK, son. I'll say no more about it, but you did the right thing."

"Jonas said something about waiting another five hundred years. Someday I may have the stomach to listen to what that lunatic raving meant."

"OK, Caleb, as you wish. Can you sit for a spell?"

"No, Pops. I'll be back later on, but for now I have some other business. I'll see you later, though."

"Good enough. I look forward to it. Again, you did what had to be done, and you did it like a man."

"Thanks, Pops. Jacob! Missy! Time to go!"

Patty looked around the corner and said "You're taking them again?"

"Yeah. I want them with me. I'll bring them back in the morning."

"You promise?", Patty asked with a genuine pout.

"I promise, little sister."

As the trio were driving home, Jacob could sense his papa's melancholy and licked Cal's hand as it rested on the shifter. Cal put his hand under Jacob and lifted the little dog onto his lap. He drove like that, with Jacob's rear paws on Cal's thighs, while Jacob's front paws were on the steering wheel. Missy, keeping her custom, stuck her head out the window, barking at leaves, rabbits, and squirrels.

CHAPTER NEXT

After Caleb deposited his pals at home in their crates so they wouldn't cut themselves on the glass that was still in the imperfectly cleaned-up house, he went back to his car and drove off. Today had made him a little harder than he was before, if that was possible, and a little more determined to put things right.

He drove to a house that lived on a lonely road on the far south side of the island. He parked on the side of the lane opposite the house.

Cal marveled at the care with which the yard was maintained. The lawn was perfectly manicured. The shrubs were trimmed with a precision used normally by watchmakers. The place looked as if it had come off the cover of a magazine. It was beautiful—on the outside. On the inside lived a man of brooding darkness, a man quite the opposite of his great-uncle Jonas.

His humanity had been rotted away from the inside eons ago. He had plunged himself into the service of a lightless, lifeless master those same eons before. He lived so that he might bring death. Death was his food, and human anguish was his drink.

The windows were covered with curtains, so Caleb could not see into the house. He knew the man was inside. He could feel it in his gut; he could smell it; he could taste it.

Cal stared at the house intently, with an almost hateful purpose, carefully staying away from hate. Hate would keep Cal from his purpose, and that purpose was the death of the man in the house. If he had to kill one of his best friends, send him "home," as Jonas had put it, he would balance the books, somehow by sending this man back to hell.

As he watched, Cal saw the curtains part as if someone had pulled them back to look out the window, but no one was visible. A long time ago, Cal had stopped being shocked by such things, though he still did not like the supernatural.

However, he was beginning to see what his purpose was, what was inside of him. That knowledge scared and thrilled him. So when the curtains dropped, Cal was not at all surprised to "know" that the man in the house was gone and would not be back again today.

He started his car and drove back to his parents' house, but not before going to the local ice-cream shop and buying four quart containers of hand-packed rocky-road ice cream for Patty.

CHAPTER HARRY

Harry Martin had been born different. There was something inside him that was untouchable. Deep inside those places that made Harry who he was, those places where only God could go, was something beautiful and horrible.

The truth of the matter was that Harry was born a demon, a real, honest-to-goodness (or badness) demon, but the rarest of demons: a demon loyal to the Creator of All Things. He did not consciously know this, of course, but somewhere deep in himself, he knew. The Evil One still felt the sting of the loss of one of his most powerful allies and still held the grudge.

Harry had a world-class intellect on par with both Caleb and Joshua. Caleb had his gifts, and Joshua, his. What Harry possessed was the ability, because of his origins, to go to very bad places and associate with very bad people; sometimes he had to do some very bad things and come away undefiled. From the times he was with Ora, to the many times he had to uncover the reasons someone had died, Harry was the man for the dirty job, though he was not a dirty man.

In fact, Harry, born and raised Catholic, was a true believer, but he was not religious in the normal sense of the word. He went to Mass on some Sundays. He thought that God was great—and he knew, somehow, that God loved him—but going to Mass was for "them that needed it."

Harry really was untouchable in that there was that thing inside him, that thing that shone as brightly as the sun but was impossible to see. That thing made him courageous where others were timid, and curious about things that made others run screaming.

As he grew, it was clear Harry was an odd kid. He was not weird, not in a way that put people off, but there was something different about him that folks could not put a finger on.

Maybe it was the way that, when he spoke to you, Harry seemed to be looking around you toward what was behind you that made people feel as if they ought to be turning around to see what was there. Maybe it was his ethereal grin; he seemed to be always just done laughing at a joke that no one else was in on.

The experience of meeting Harry for the first time was like walking through a door to an alternate universe where things were almost, but not quite, the same as in the one you had just left.

Harry had a bright and engaging smile and wide, curious eyes. His hair was always disheveled, always unkempt, but somehow he always managed to smell good and look good. Harry was very clean, just a slob. He was popular with girls, who always wanted to date him, and with boys, who always wanted to hang out with him for what might happen next.

Harry was afraid of nothing that others would term spooky. His whole existence seemed to be for the sole purpose of saying, "No matter how ugly or evil things look, I'm not afraid."

If Harry had been in the woods and come across an abandoned—and to a twelve-year-old mind, clearly haunted—house, he would have run into the old house to see what secrets it held, and further, he would have turned the experience into a chapter in his journal titled "Who's Afraid of the Big, Bad Haunted House? Not I."

There were several old cemeteries on North Island, very creepy, all with weathered headstones that have skulls engraved on them reading "...in the year of Our Lord..." While other kids would whistle past the cemeteries on gloomy nights, Harry would walk into them, looking and poking around, wondering what the corpses, hundreds of years old, looked like now. Harry was the living personification of the person in the movies who runs down to the dark basement to check out what could have made that bloodcurdling scream.

Just after Caleb and Joshua had their incident with Ora on their walk home from school, when all three boys were teenagers, Harry convinced the Catholic parish, the town, and his family to let him exhume an ancestor 350 years deceased so that a postmortem could be performed on the man's remains.

Harry was in his glory. He went to the cemetery the day permission was granted and said to his ancestor Lemuel Martin, "Grandpa Lem, today is the day. Today we start to find out, maybe, who or what killed you. It's been three hundred fifty years, and I know that's a long time to wait for anything, but I promise you that we will get to the bottom of this."

Harry had been in correspondence with a professor of archeology and forensics at Boston College for a while before he got the idea for the dig. The professor was a Dr. Exaro Romano, MD, PhD.

Dr. Romano had been very encouraging to Harry, so when Harry told the professor of his idea for a dig, the professor was very eager to see it happen.

The good professor and three of his graduate students came to the island to lend guidance and do their own research. Exhumation had not happened before on North Island, and the academic world was interested in what lay in the grave. There were long-standing questions about the early settlement of the island

and questions regarding several unsolved murders that had happened under mysterious circumstances.

On the day the dig was supposed to begin, a terrible storm, a real "nor'eastah," blew over the island. Harry was very upset and wanted to go to the graveyard to dig even if there was a storm outside. His father, though indulgent regarding his son's unconventional interests, was not about to let his son go out on a day when the weather presented a danger to life and limb.

Three days of rain nearly put Harry 'round the bend, but on the fourth day, the sun shone, and the sky was a brilliant blue. The day was cold, but not outrageously so. It would have been a perfect day for a dig, but the ground needed to dry out a bit. After a few more days of dry weather, things were ready and falling into place.

Professor Romano arrived at the Martin house early, but not early enough to catch Harry sleeping. Harry had been up at five and was already out at the cemetery, marking the site with strings and stakes. He laid out a grid, setting up everything just right for the dig.

The grave that Harry wanted to dig up was not just a random choice. Harry had been reading about the history of the island and found out that throughout the entire history of North Island—and not just since it was settled by Europeans, but from the very first Native settlers—there had been many reports of unnatural deaths. Native legends told of a white witch who came in the night to eat men's souls.

White histories were so similar to the Native descriptions that most historians put it down to the European settlers appropriating Native stories and retelling them. The murders, if that is truly what they were, were gratuitously bloody, all butchery, as if the murders were simply a vehicle to convey just how much hatred existed in the killers themselves.

Harry had shown his research to his closest friends, Caleb and Joshua. The two boys were very interested in the material that

Harry had found, and Caleb in particular found himself fascinated by the fact that dozens and dozens of people over more than one thousand years had been murdered without one single incident being solved.

Caleb asked, "Hey, Harry, what is this about Lemuel's body being found in a church?"

Joshua's ears perked up.

"Yeah," Harry said. "From what I can see, he was found in the Catholic church—what else? —kneeling in a pew, with a broken rosary in his hands. Most of the beads and the crucifix were on the floor beneath him."

Harry saw the hair on Josh's arm stand up. Josh asked, "Was anything else there? Does what you have read say if there was anything else there with Lemuel?"

"Like what?"

"Well, like anything that ought not to have been there."

Harry looked pensive for a moment. "Aside from a dead body kneeling in a church, I'm not sure." Harry laughed. He looked at Caleb, who was smiling at the quip, and then to Joshua, who was not smiling. He said in a more serious tone, "I dunno, but I'll look into it, Josh."

Later that day, Harry went to the school library to see if there was anything more that he could find out about his ancestor. There was nothing more in the little library, and the island was too small to support a public library. So he went to his original source, the Roman Catholic Archdiocese of Boston archive.

CHAPTER BILLY AND COLLIN

Collin McIntyre and Billy Driscoll were the best of friends. They had been best friends for years and years and years. At least in their minds it had been that long. Billy and Collin were thirteen and so had been friends for years if you did not go back too far.

The boys were adventurers and amateur spelunkers and loved tramping about the island in places they ought not to be—places that were dangerous.

On this day, Billy and Collin were out adventuring in the deep woods of North Island when it began to snow. It was very early for snow and cold weather. Autumn was only a few weeks old, but their island, a dot fifty miles off the coast, was not a place where anything, especially weather, was predictable. The snow was welcome at first. Maybe there would be a snow day at school tomorrow. So the boys marched on, not noticing the flakes falling faster and harder.

About an hour into their hike, Collin looked up and said, "Hey, Bill, where are we? I don't recognize any of the trees, and we've lost our trail." This was very weird to Collin, because they had been taught well by their fathers about tracking. They had been over every uninhabited inch of their island and could tell one trail from another, one nearly identical tree from another, just by looking at the lichens that grew on it. They could tell what part of the island they were on by the smells in the breeze.

Billy had been tracking a deer for some time, a large, heavy buck by the looks of its tracks, and was so engrossed that he did not hear Collin speaking to him.

Collin raised his voice. "*Billy*, stop tracking that stupid deer and listen to me. Do you recognize this part of the forest? Because I don't."

Billy, who was as good a woodsman as Collin, looked up at him and said, "C'mon, Coll, we could blindfold each other and find our way home. For Christ's sake, we could smell our way home. Whaddya mean you don't rec…" and then his voice trailed off, because he realized with a nauseating pain in his gut that Collin was right.

CHAPTER NEXT

In another part of the forest, not too far away from the boys, stood another tracker, confused and a little sick to his stomach.

Edgerton Alchurch, MD, island doctor, had been tracking a deer, a deer whose tracks told him that it was a big buck. For more than an hour he had followed it, never seeing it, and now he was more than a little frustrated. The newly falling snow was not helping as it covered the tracks he was following.

So when he decided that the buck would have to wait until tomorrow, he stopped and looked up for the first time in some twenty minutes. He propped his shotgun, a Belgian Browning that had been his father's, against one of the trees and tried to get his bearings.

Dr. Alchurch, except his years spent in college, medical school and a stint in the USMC as a surgeon during Operation Desert Storm, had spent his entire life on North Island. Indeed, he'd been born in a cabin that had stood not too far from where he thought he was. The problem he had at that moment was that he did not know where he was. For a man who had spent many a day hunting in these very woodlands, that was a very disconcerting feeling.

Then Dr. Alchurch smelled burning oak and hickory. When he looked above the tree line, he saw, through the falling flakes, smoke rising in a column as if from a chimney.

This gave him a small sense of relief. The trees were still unrecognizable, and in his agitation, he did not stop to think that there shouldn't be an inhabited cabin anywhere near here. He picked up his shotgun, walked forward in the direction of the smoke, and in a few minutes, came upon a cabin identical to the one in which he'd been raised.

Alchurch looked at the cabin, perfect in every detail, and felt a tightness in his chest. His family's cabin had burned down many years ago, the victim of a forest fire started by lightning. Even the top layer of the foundation stones was eventually carted away for other uses.

He approached the cabin's front porch, the supporting beams of which had been hewn from felled trees, stripped of their bark, and used in their natural shapes. Alchurch put his left hand on the front door and pushed it open. There never had been a doorknob or any lock on it. His family lived out in the woods, after all.

As the door opened, Dr. Alchurch saw the crackling fire, the table set for dinner with the enameled steel plates his mother had used for years.

In the center of the table was a fresh venison roast. In three bowls arranged about the roast were potatoes, carrots, and turnips, all grown by the family.

Dr. Alchurch put his shotgun up against the wall by the doorway, where it had stood for years when he was a child. He walked over to the chair that had been his when he was a boy and sat down.

The fire crackled and popped, the smell of venison wafted to his nose, and then he saw her. She stood in the space between the kitchen, with its woodstove cooker, and the room where Alchurch sat.

CHAPTER NEXT

The figure of Edgerton Alchurch's mother stood before him, looking as warm and loving as he had remembered her to be. Alchurch sat in the chair, rigid and speechless, looking at his mother's face. He did not know if he should be scared or happy. The figure of his mother made not a move toward him. She looked at him and smiled. Alchurch could feel the warmth of her smile, and he began to cry, letting out a pain that had been fermenting for some fifty years.

"Son, my son." Alchurch heard words from the figure of his mother, though her mouth did not move. The loving gleam in her eyes never changed.

"My son, I have always been with you. Your father has always been with you." With that, Alchurch's father appeared behind his mother. His father was not smiling but rather had a look of absolute peace and understanding.

Alchurch heard the voice of his father the same way he had heard his mother. His mouth did not move. His tones were loving and gentle but also strong, solid, filled with purpose. "You came here not by accident, my dearest son. We brought you here, both of us, to give you our message."

So far, Edgerton Alchurch had been silent, not knowing what to make of any of it. Now he spoke. "What message, Father?" was all he could manage.

His mother's voice said, "Billy needs you. Do you understand?"

"No. No, I don't. I don't know a Billy. What do you mean? Wait—do you mean the Driscoll boy?"

Instead of answering, Mrs. Alchurch simply stood in the doorway, saying not a word.

Alchurch looked at his father. "Father, what does any of this mean?"

His father spoke without a muscle in his peaceful face moving a fraction of an inch.

"Soon you will understand."

"Father, Mother..." He could not say another word.

The figures of his parents started to grow diaphanous. He stood and shouted, "No! Don't go! I've waited so long. I've missed you both so much."

"My son," his mother said, "we will always be with you. We have never left your side."

His father said, "Be strong, my son. Our departure was necessary for you to become the man you are now." And they were gone.

The cold Darkness had taken note of what had just happened. *This must not be*, thought the Darkness.

Edgerton Alchurch stood in silence as the figures of his parents faded from his sight. From the fireplace, a flaming log rolled out onto the floor and across the small room, stopping just under the heavy curtains at the front of the house.

In seconds, the curtains were ablaze. Smoke filled the room. Alchurch made for the door, but as he got to it, the door slammed shut and would not open. He pulled with all of his strength. In a minute he was overcome by the smoke. He slumped to the floor as the cabin burned around him.

Alchurch opened his eyes. They stung, as if irritated by smoke. He was on his back, his shotgun by his side, and could see snowflakes drifting lazily down through the branches onto his face. He should have been cold but wasn't. He should have been sore but wasn't. He should have been dead but wasn't. He could not remember how he had gotten there.

Dr. Alchurch stood up feebly. Through his stinging eyes, he looked about him to see his familiar forest. This brought him an overwhelming sense of relief. He saw the trail that he knew so very well being quickly covered by the falling snow. That did not matter. He could see the trees, and they were familiar friends. He could get home from here.

CHAPTER NEXT

"Wait just one second," Billy yelled out to the woods as he looked around him in disbelief. "What the fuck is going on around here?"

Billy glared at Collin. Swearing was not something that Billy did easily. His language took Collin aback. Collin, who usually spoke in a torrent of "fucks" and "shits," looked back in surprise at Billy. "How the fuckin' hell am I supposed to know? We are fuckin' lost."

"That's what I'm asking, Coll. How did we, of all the kids on North Island, get lost? I, we, haven't been lost in these woods, ever…before now."

"I don't know, Bill. I don't know how we managed to get lost, but here we are. No use getting crazy over it until we find out what's up."

"Then we can get crazy over it, I suppose?" Billy replied.

"No, not even then. You know what our fathers taught us. Keep your head, and you'll keep your life. So we're gonna keep our heads. OK?"

"OK. I've never lost my cool in the woods before. Don't plan to start now." Billy said. He turned his face upward. "Hey, Coll, do you smell that?"

Collin smelled the cold air. "It's burning wood, but I don't see any smoke."

"Well, Coll, the tracks of that buck are getting lost in the snow, but I can still see them. Let's keep going. Maybe we'll find out where we are."

"All right. Let's go," Collin said, and off they went, following the tracks of the large deer.

Dr. Alchurch turned in the direction of the trail and started to walk back out of the woods toward where he had left his truck. About half a mile down the trail, he felt the urge to stop, though he did not know why. As he stood on the path wondering what he should do, Alchurch heard the howl of a wolf. His blood froze in his veins. The last wolf on North Island was shot more than 150 years before.

He snapped to and started walking, quickly, back from where he came. As he followed the trail back to where he had woken up, he noticed that his footprints were not the only ones in the snow. Next to his prints, and pointing in the direction of where the cabin had been, were the footprints of a very large wolf. Being that the island's year-round population was small, Alchurch also served as the community's ersatz veterinarian. These tracks were not of any dog, he was positive of that. He was beyond being surprised at this point, but the sight of the tracks prodded him to walk faster and faster back along the trail.

Billy and Collin followed the tracks of the buck for some minutes until they came to a clearing in the woods. There, in the center of the clearing, stood the charred remains of a stone foundation. The boys walked up to the snowy stones, and it was clear to them that the building that had been there had burned down many years ago.

Billy said, "Coll, do you smell that?"

Collin replied, "Yeah, Bill, I smell it. Burned wood. Burned, like, an hour ago, but this house didn't burn down an hour ago."

"Nope. It didn't."

"So what gives?"

The two boys had positioned themselves so that they were on opposite sides of the foundation.

Billy looked up at Collin and said, "Things been weird since we got into this part of the island. I dunno why this ought to be any different."

"This is different; this is very different. I'm not sure why, but it is. I've got a very bad feeling about this."

"You've got a bad feeling now? Jesus, Coll. How many weird things have to happen before you get a bad feeling?"

Collin, pointing at the ruins, said, "This many."

Dr. Alchurch was in a run by now. The wolf tracks were still visible beneath the snow cover, but sometimes it sounded to the doctor as if the wolf were behind him, following him. *No, not following*, he thought, *chasing*.

He looked over his shoulder but could see nothing. His heart was racing, more from fear than from running. He could hear his breathing in his ears and could sense the sound of the wolf behind him, hunting him.

When he was fifty yards from where the cabin had stood, he saw two boys standing on either side of the remains of his boyhood home. He recognized them. Everyone on the island was a patient of his, and he knew these two boys well.

He called, "Willy, Collin!" The doctor was the only one on the island to call Billy "Willy."

From his right shoulder came a searing pain. A gray wolf, impossibly big, sank its teeth into him with a horrible fury. Alchurch dropped to the ground, and before he started his roll, in a move he had learned in the Corps, he shoved the barrels of his shotgun between his arm and body behind him and pulled both triggers at once.

The wolf forced out one last gurgling growl, its mouth went slack, and it dropped to the ground. His momentum carried him back onto his feet, and in an automatic move, being too pumped with adrenaline to feel much of the pain, Alchurch broke the gun at the breech and loaded two more shells. He thought that his military experience had been worthwhile as he kept running toward the boys.

Alchurch saw another giant wolf leap at Collin, taking the boy down into the hole of the cellar. Alchurch himself leaped into the hole, and as he landed on the wolf tearing at the flesh of the terrified boy, he brought the butt of the gun down on the animal's head while at the same time firing one of the barrels straight into the air. The force of Alchurch bringing the stock down on the wolf's head combined with the force of the gun's recoil was enough to stun the beast. The doctor and the wolf fell to the floor. Alchurch scrambled to his feet, and before the wolf could gather itself, he placed one shell's worth of number-two buckshot square in the wolf's face.

There was no time to see to Collin's condition as a third wolf landed on the dirt floor with Billy's arm, Billy still attached, firmly in its jaws. The doctor reloaded again, as he felt a wave of weakness come over him. Both barrels discharged, wolf dispatched, he passed out face first in the dirt.

Collin rose to his feet, and not too steadily. Billy was, by now, kneeling on the ground holding his right arm with his left, vomiting from the pain. Collin managed to stagger over to Billy, who said to Collin, though weakly, "I'll be OK. Go see to the doc."

Collin went the couple of feet over to where Dr. Alchurch was lying, crouched down beside him, and turned the doctor onto his back. Collin hadn't noticed in the excitement, but the wolf that had attacked Alchurch had nearly torn off his arm. The doctor was bleeding badly, so Collin took the doctor's scarf from around his neck, took off his own coat and sweatshirt, and with them made a rough tourniquet to try to stanch the bleeding.

Billy had stopped throwing up and now stood next to Collin and the doctor. Billy's own wounds were extensive, so Collin got up and said to him, "Lemme look at that." Coll pulled away the remaining fabric from Billy's plaid woolen hunting jacket to reveal a not-so-clean slice through the flesh down to the bone.

"OK," Billy said, "how does it look?"

"Well, it looks pretty good," Collin lied. "But don't try to move it, OK?"

Billy looked down at his arm. "It doesn't hurt for some reason. I wonder why." Then he passed out on the dirt floor next to the doctor.

Collin looked down at the two figures lying in the dirt and said aloud to himself, "How am I going to get you two out of here?" He sat down next to Billy and the doctor, putting his hand on Billy's shoulder just above the gaping wound.

What had just happened started to sink in: losing their way, crazy; the burned-out foundation that they had never seen before, crazy; being attacked by giant wolves—well, there were no words for how fucked up that was, he thought. Collin began to feel a little woozy. His mind could not take it all in. Then he remembered his father's words. "Keep your head, and you'll keep your life." So Collin frowned, squashed down the wooziness, suppressed his confusion, and stood up to assess the situation—not to understand what had happened, but to figure out what to do next. He looked around him and up to the sky. No branches above to try to grab. In any event, there wasn't any rope to throw around a branch that wasn't there. He searched the dirt floor. There was nothing. No wood planks, no old beams...nothing. He couldn't jury-rig anything to help himself and his friends out of the old cellar. Then an idea struck him. Collin walked back to his two injured friends and, as carefully as he could, dragged each one by his ankles to one side of the basement.

He was only thirteen, so he struggled mightily with Dr. Alchurch, but he had an easier time with Billy. Both moaned with pain on being moved but did not come to.

Collin went to the wall opposite where the doctor and Billy lay, took his Bowie knife from its scabbard, and began to pry mortar from between the ancient stones. When enough mortar had been chipped away, Collin found it easy to pull the stone out and let it fall to the ground.

He jammed his knife behind the adjacent stone and pried, and it, too, fell to the dirt floor. The next five stones were easy enough, and now he stood beside a pile of stones, staring at the dirt wall behind them, still showing the shovel marks from the time the basement was dug.

He looked the wall over and saw that removing one more stone might send the entire thing crumbling to the floor. Collin put his knife behind the chosen stone, pried it away, watched it fall on top of the pile, then stepped back and waited. The wall shifted a tiny bit. Collin took another step back. The wall shifted a little more. He held his breath. Then, in one big move, the stones avalanched down into a pile that would let Collin climb up and out of the cellar. He climbed the pile of stones, balancing carefully on the unstable rocks. When he made it to the top, he wondered how he would get Billy and the doctor out and to medical attention, especially when Dr. Alchurch was the medical attention. Neither he nor Billy was allowed a cell phone. Their parents did not like what they saw cell phones doing to the culture. *Damn it*, he thought, *the doctor must have one.*

Collin scrambled down the pile and searched the doc's jacket pockets and found, to his great happiness, an iPhone. He sighed with relief. The relief did not last when he saw that the thing would not turn on. The battery was dead.

Collin sat down next to the doc and Billy, reminded himself to keep his head, and thought. From above him and a little distance away, he heard a low growling and leaped for the doctor's shotgun. He pointed it at the sky, expecting a wolf to come charging down upon them. His hands were trembling a little, and he accidentally pulled the rear trigger on the gun and…nothing.

That's right, he thought. *The doc unloaded one barrel into the sky and one into that wolf right over there.* Collin turned to look where the dead wolf lay. It was gone.

Keeping his father's counsel was getting a little more difficult, but he managed to calm himself down and reached into to the doctor's hunting coat, pulled out two twelve-gauge shotgun shells, and loaded them into the breech of the gun.

In the excitement, he had not noticed that the snow had stopped falling. Now he noticed. In his head he recalled his mother's voice saying, "Thank goodness for small favors." He looked over at his two friends. They had lost a lot of blood, but the tourniquets had worked; the bleeding had stopped.

The McIntyre and Driscoll families had begun to notice the fading daylight. It really wasn't odd for the boys to be out all day and even to camp out overnight. However, if they wanted to stay out in the woods overnight, they had had strict instructions from both sets of parents to let them know what their plans were. Right at this moment, both sets of parents were beginning to rethink the whole "no cell phone" thing.

Bill Driscoll Sr. picked up the phone, a 1954 Ma Bell Bakelite model, and dialed his friend's house.

"John? Hey, this is Bill."

"Hey, Bill. Was thinking of calling you."

"I guess that means you haven't seen the boys, either. It's getting late, and I'm getting a little worried."

"No, Bill. Haven't seen them since this morning when they left here to go tracking on the far side of the island."

"Yep, that's what Billy told me that he and Coll were going to do. I'm glad, at least, that their stories match up."

John McIntyre laughed into the phone. "I guess they're smarter than we were at their age. How many times did we get caught out in a lie because we couldn't keep our stories straight?"

"Too many times for my sore behind, John. Too many times. Look, how about you get Rosey and I'll get Ben, and we'll let 'em sniff a shirt or something. Then maybe we can track them."

"OK, I'll get Rosey ready, and we'll be at your place in fifteen, twenty minutes."

"Good. See you in a few, John."

John McIntyre and Bill Driscoll, led by Rosey and Ben, a red-bone coonhound and a bloodhound, respectively, were fading deep into the woods behind the Driscolls' cabin, tracking their sons.

Their feet crunched through the snow, and they were both glad to see that the falling snow had given way to a clear sky. That was both good and bad. The less snow, the easier the boys would be to track, but the clear sky meant a much colder night. That could be bad.

William Driscoll, John McIntyre, Rosey, and Ben wove their way through the trees. The trees, for their part, silently acknowledged their old friends. John and Bill felt that familiarity inside themselves. Outwardly, neither one professed any kind of religious, spiritual, or mystical beliefs, but a deeper part of them knew. It just knew.

So not only the dogs but the trees guided them on their way. To the dogs, the guidance of the trees, the wind, the ground on which they walked were givens, as taken for granted as breathing. The men could sense only a nudge in this direction or that.

The men and the dogs marched on in silence for some time before John spoke to distract himself from the fear that he felt for the boys. "Do you remember, Bill, when we were kids, we would go tracking all over this island? My pop told me to never go to one part of North Island, and that's just where our boys were going. They told me so."

Bill was glad, too, to take his mind off the thoughts charging around his brain. "I know. The Devil's Graveyard. Billy had been talking about this trek for days. I knew that he and Collin had at least been thinking about exploring that part of the island."

"So do you put any stock in what our fathers told us?"

"No, no. I don't. Or I didn't. But I've got a queasy feeling in my gut, and now I don't know what to think."

"Look, our fathers taught us many valuable things: how to hunt, fish, track, and survive in the wilderness—not just here but all over the Northeast. You know how many trips we went on just in Maine alone?"

"Can't say as I recall that number."

"Well, I do. Starting from we were four until they died, our fathers took us to the deep Maine woods twenty-three times."

"You always did have a head for the detail, John."

"And you for the big picture. Funny how that seems to have been reversed in our sons."

"Old friend, you know exactly why that is."

John looked at his friend with a knowing grin. "Yes, I do, old boy. Yes, I do."

Their lighthearted moment was cut off by the dogs catching the scent of the boys.

"OK, they've been through here." Bill looked down to the forest floor to see what only a seasoned tracker's eyes could make out: some broken sticks, looking like all the other broken sticks around them; some crushed leaves, looking no different from any other leaves on the ground. But to John and Bill, these things told a story of who walked this way, when, and in what direction they were headed.

By now, it was fully dark in the thick of the woods, and the men stopped to open their packs and pull out head-mounted lights. They made good time, but it was getting very cold. When they were about three-quarters of a mile from the Graveyard, they stopped to put small boots on their dogs' feet.

As Bill and John stood up and their lights pointed to the canopy of the forest for a moment, they were both scared to silence by what they saw: a body, a skeleton, hanging from a cord, dangling in the light breeze that blew through the trees. John backed up a step and tripped over his dog. Bill bent over to help him up out of the snow.

When the two men pointed their lights to where the body hung, it was gone.

John gathered himself, brushing the snow from his trousers. He walked over to the spot under which they had seen the body, only to see bloodstained snow. Bill followed him, both dogs in tow, and shone his light down at the snow.

Bill said, "I don't know what that was, and I don't care. We've got to find our sons *now!*"

"Let's get the hell out of here," John replied. With that, John's cell phone, the one he kept "just in case," began to ring, and both men let out a yell of "Jezuussss Christ!". The dogs began to bark uncontrollably in response.

"It's only my phone, Bill; it's only my phone." John took the phone from his jacket pocket. "Rosey, Ben, quiet now. Quiet." He opened the old flip phone.

The voice on the other end said, "John, this is Sheriff Parsons. I called your place to invite you and Bill hunting and she told me that you and Bill are out looking for your boys."

Bill tapped John on the shoulder and pointed to the ground under where the body had hung. John looked over, and his eyes got big. There was nothing there. The snow was pristine, without even a footprint on it. John's mouth was agape. He said nothing into the phone for several seconds.

The sheriff said, "John, you there? John?"

"Uh, yeah, Aleksi, I'm still here. The boys, they went out this morning and never came back. We got worried and have gone after them. Nothing yet, though." John looked over at Bill, who was pointing up and making a cutting motion with his hand across his neck.

John knew what his friend meant and agreed—no mentioning the body hanging in the tree, the body that was no longer there, the crimson snow that was now white. They had enough trouble for the moment.

"Well, I've got some more trouble for you, John. Doc Alchurch is missing, too. He told his nurse, after office hours last night, that he was going hunting in the Graveyard this morning. He has not been heard from. I'd come out to help you, but I'm the only one on duty and I have to be available in case anything else happens around here."

"I understand. That's not good news about the Doc. Damn it! OK, Al, I'll tell Bill. We'd better go. Got to find those boys and the doc."

"Keep me informed if you find anything."

John looked at Bill and then to the tree where they had seen the body. Had he and Bill had been hallucinating? Couldn't be. They'd both seen it. "You bet, Sheriff." He folded the phone into his pocket.

John sighed a long, tired breath. "The Doc went hunting in the Graveyard this morning, and no one knows where he is."

Bill looked sick. "If there is one man who knows this island and all the forests of the Northeast as well as we do, it's Doc Alchurch. Fuck it all, John, he grew up in the graveyard."

The dogs were getting agitated. It was full dark by now, and the moon shone bright in the sky. Bill rubbed his temples with his free hand. This was going from serious to potentially tragic.

The two men, led by the two dogs, trudged forward in silence, both men afraid to say what was on their minds: that if Doc Alchurch, a man as skilled as they, could go missing, then, well, it was not worth contemplating.

Collin knew that he had but a few minutes to get some sort of fire started. His mind kicked into gear, and he remembered his training. He took all the things out of his coat pockets: the compasses, his small knife, a spool of heavy thread, and a leather case with just as heavy sewing needles. But the most important thing was the steel-and-flint fire starter.

Collin bunched up the coat, said a small Indian prayer that he had read about in *Boys' Life* magazine, and struck the flint with the steel next to part of the lining of the coat.

He had to get this fire going, because now he had only a light jacket and his thermals to ward off the growing bitterness.

Damn it, he thought, It's not catching. Collin stood up and hugged himself against the cold. He looked up, and from above came gusts of wind hitting him in the face in rhythmic fashion. At the same time, he felt a warmth come from inside himself, and he stopped shivering.

Collin turned to the pile of stones that he had pulled from the wall and climbed to the top. He walked around to the other side of the hole and looked around. He walked a few feet and found a spot where the snow looked like it had been blown away by a fast wind. In the center of the clearing was what Collin estimated to be about half a cord of firewood and several piles of sticks.

"This is weird." Then, thinking of what they all had been through in the last few hours, he realized that weird was the new normal, and he smiled and was proud that he had handled everything that had come his way.

There was no time for self-congratulation, though. It was cold and dark, and there were two people lying down in that hole. He was not sure they would live the night if they had to spend it out here. That thought scared him a little.

Collin picked up the nearest pile of kindling and held it under his left arm. Then he went over to the firewood and chose one of the smaller logs. He hurried to the side of the hole and climbed back down. He arranged the kindling in a little teepee formation about five feet from the doc and Billy and placed the log against one side.

Collin clambered up the rocks again to fetch two more logs. He reached the top of the hole and ran over to the logs. As he put his hands on the wood, he saw out of the corner of his eye a faint light coming from the bottom of the hole. Collin grabbed the split logs and made his way, like a shot, over to the rock pile.

When he got to the edge of the hole, he could see that the sticks were aflame. He scrambled down the rocks as fast as he could and stood there in front of the small fire, his mouth agape. The little fire began to burn itself out, so Collin snapped out of his trance, ran back up the hill of rocks, grabbed more sticks, scrambled down the hole again and put them on the fire. The flames grew large again, and Collin placed the three split logs over the burning sticks and then went to get more kindling. Having done that, he watched the flames lick at the logs until they caught fire, too.

Three more trips up and down the rock pile, and there was a blaze that would keep them warm for a couple of hours with a small pile of split logs in reserve. Collin walked over to the figures lying in the flickering light.

He checked on the doc and Billy. They were warm and breathing, but they had both lost a lot of blood. This was not good. Collin sat down next to them, and a wave of fatigue washed over him. In minutes, he was sleeping, with his head resting on his rolled-up coat.

Above, a conflagrant winged figure stood watch over the man and boys. From an unfathomable distance came the howls of hungry wolves. The figure raised a fiery hand, and the howls fell silent.

Men and dogs plowed through the snow in silence. The only sounds to be heard were from the dogs as they pulled on the scent as if it were a rope tied to the boys.

A full minute before the men caught it, the dogs, smelling the smoke from the fire, broke the leashes free from Bill's grip and charged forward into the darkness, yelping and barking as they went.

"Get your asses back here, goddamn it! This is all we need, the dogs chasing after a raccoon or some such. Damn it, let's find those dogs, John."

John and Bill started to jog but got only about ten feet before John grabbed Bill's arm. "Stop, stop, Bill. Do you smell that?"

Bill, who was a bit more agitated because he was blaming himself for not holding on to the dogs, stopped. A look of surprise and joy came over his face. "Smoke! I smell smoke!"

John smiled. "Hold on. I can hear the dogs!"

"I don't hear anyth—good fucking God, I hear them, too," Bill said.

Collin was in more than a deep sleep as he lay next to the fire. He was only thirteen years old, and his body and mind had been through battle.

He had fought hard, well beyond his years, and had won. In winning, though, he had used up everything he had, and his system had gone into something akin to a coma to conserve energy and put what little resources remained into healing.

Collin was deep in a dream. He was standing in the main hallway of his small school. Standing in front of him were Doc Alchurch and Billy. They were smiling at him. The doc approached him, put a hand on Collin's shoulder, and said, "You've done a magnificent job, son. You ought to be proud of yourself. You saved me and young Willy, here." He motioned behind him to where Billy Driscoll stood with a big stupid grin on his face.

Collin, a puzzled look on his own face, looked up at the doc. He looked around the doc to Billy. "Bill, what is he talking about? I saved you? What does he mean?"

Billy walked over to Collin. Doctor Alchurch moved aside. Collin saw the same stupid grin on the doc's face.

Billy said, "It's not important now. Just know that you are the best friend that a guy could ever ask for. We will be brothers, all three of us, for as long we live, and longer than that."

Collin looked up at the doc and then at Billy. "I think you've both been smelling fumes. What are you two talking about?"

The doc and Billy ignored the question, and the doc said, pointing at the classroom door in front of him, "There's someone in there who wants to see you. She's been waiting a long time, and it's not polite to keep a girl waiting."

Collin turned toward the door and saw, through the glass pane, Anna Marie Roget sitting on a desk. She was wearing a white dress, one that Collin had very much liked on her when she had worn it to school, and she had a red ribbon tied around her neck with a little rose medallion hanging from it.

Billy nudged Collin from behind. "Go on, Coll. You've been waiting for this moment since we were ten years old."

Collin swallowed hard but did not say anything. He looked back to Billy, who said, "Go on. There's not much time."

Collin walked to the door and opened it. The room smelled strongly of roses. Anna looked at him, and she had that same grin on her face. On Anna, though, it did not look stupid.

Anna shoved herself off the desk and approached Collin, taking his hands in hers.

"Collin McIntyre, you are the bravest, most courageous, most handsome boy in the world. I have loved you always, and I will love you forever."

Collin looked at her in amazement, and he felt a pain in his stomach that somehow did not hurt.

He looked straight into her eyes and said in a voice barely above a whisper, "Anna, I love you, too. Someday I'm gonna marry you."

Anna looked right back into his eyes and giggled. "Of course you are, silly. We've been married since before time was, and we will be married when time is no more. But for now, I have to go. Here is something to remember me by, even though you will see me day after tomorrow." With that, she leaned into Collin and kissed him softly on his lips.

Collin put his arms around her thin waist, pulled her even closer, like the guys in the movies, and kissed her right back. Anna melted in his arms for a few seconds, then pulled her head away. Then she shocked Collin even more when she leaned back in and started licking his face up and down until he was a slobbery mess.

From behind him, he heard his father's voice calling, "Collin, Collin, I'm here. Mr. Driscoll is here. Wake up, son, wake up."

Collin saw the room around him begin to fade away. Anna stepped back and said, "I'll see you the day after tomorrow, just like I said. You wait and see." Then the room and Anna were gone, and Collin was floating in inky blackness.

John McIntyre shook his son, while Bill Driscoll knelt beside his own son and began administering first aid.

Collin sailed through the blackness faster and faster until he saw his father in the distance. His eyes snapped open, and he gasped for air just in time for Rosey, who had been licking his face for five full minutes, to accidentally stick her tongue in his mouth. Then it all went black again.

Collin opened his eyes. He did not know where he was. A figure stood up from a chair in the corner and came over to him.

Anna Roget took his left hand in hers and started crying. "Collin, Collin! I've been here for two days, waiting for you to wake up!"

"Anna? Is that you? Are you really here?"

"Yes, it is really me. I've been here waiting for you to wake up."

Collin said, "Wow. Where am I? And where's my dad?"

Anna pointed to the bed on Collin's right. "This is Massachusetts General Hospital in Boston, and your dad is right over there. He stayed awake for as long as he could. He was so worried about you.

Then he collapsed on that bed about an hour ago. Your mom is across the hall with the Driscolls. Billy and Doc Alchurch are in the ICU."

Collin's eyes got big. "Holy cow. Now I remember a little. Only a little. Billy and I were tracking in the woods. After that I can't remember anything. Are they going to be OK?"

"Yes, Coll, they will be OK, but it was iffy for a while."

CHAPTER NEXT

O ra was dressed in an oversized black hoodie sweatshirt pulled over a black thermal top, and oversized flannel-lined black denim jeans.

She sat on a bench that was itself sitting on a cold and windy beach on North Island. She was not happy. Her father, her master, had given her a task, and she had failed. The punishment for her failure had been horrific. The physical punishment had been the least of it.

The gashes across her back and thighs had bled for hours, as her master had not yet allowed the healing that a being of her level would normally experience.

So even now her wounds seeped blood into the dressings she had created from literally nothing by dint of sheer will and focus. The black clothing reflected what was inside her and had the added benefit of not showing the blood that leaked past the dressings.

Worse than the pain of her physical wounds were the mental and emotional torture her master had inflicted on her. Ora's master had removed her from the world, had removed her from herself.

All of her psychological landmarks had been removed, and she was sent spinning, falling into infinity. She was sent into a dizzy, twisting sickness that seemed to never end. She was in this horror for an unknown period, though it felt like forever.

Now she sat on the bench in the lotus position, middle fingertips pressed lightly against thumb tips, meditating. She meditated for focus and for relief of the physical pain she still felt. She meditated to calm the swirling nausea that churned her stomach.

Goddamn this, she thought, breaking her focus. *A being such as I am should not have to endure this.* "Master, father," she murmured, "I know that I failed you and made you angry, and for that I wish I could be sorry, but goddamn you, I am not."

She refocused, and her meditation continued. The cold, salty November breeze blew her perfect blond hair. As she meditated, the time around her slowed until it was but a drip from the tap of the future.

In this slowed state, her concentration became a sharp chisel on the stone of reality, and she could form it into whatever she liked, without interference from her master for the moment.

Doing this required solitude, a certain connection with the Earth, and very pointed attention. While in this state, she found that she could stanch the bleeding and heal her wounds.

The focus of her thoughts changed from her own lessening pain to the hatred she was birthing for her master. They had never been close in the human sense of the term and were not physically related in the human sense of that term, either, but they were related on a much deeper, closer level than one human could be related to another. Indeed, she herself had been birthed from her master's cold and directed hatred.

As she sat, her conscious mind cut its moorings from her physical body, and she let herself drift freely on the unseen currents of thought that weave the fabric of the everyday world. She knew that, if she kept a picture in her mind's eye, those currents would take her to the place or thing represented in the picture.

Presently, a building came into view. This was no random building. It was a hospital, Massachusetts General Hospital. From her vantage point she could also see three terrifying winged figures. Their form was familiar to her, as it represented her own native form. However, even to her, an Angel dark, an Angel cold, an Angel empty, an Angel of unimaginable power, these beings were frightening to behold. They appeared to her as a conflagration of blue flame with wings of pure light, all raging with tightly controlled fury.

In a fit of very bad judgment, she hurled spears of hate at the fiery beings before her. They took no notice. She screamed at them, "Angels of the Lord! Soldiers of God! Holy Warriors of the Heavenly Host! Hear me!"

The three Angels took no notice. She held in her mind the picture of the three she had failed to kill some days before. She found herself looking down through the roof of the hospital on Collin McIntyre, Billy Driscoll, and Dr. Edgerton Alchurch.

Once again, she directed her thought. She took out knives, carved her thought into daggers, and hurled them at the three lying in their beds.

Her focus widened, and time nearly froze in place. With time leaking by, she could watch her daggers of hate sail toward their victims. She let her grip on time loosen, and the daggers shot off like bullets. The daggers hit the doctor, Billy, and Collin. She watched as the weapons exploded in their targets. A great satisfaction washed over her as she watched what she was certain were the deaths of the three parasites who had caused her so much trouble in the woods.

The blinding light of the explosions faded, and she looked to see three corpses lying in their hospital beds. But, to her horror, Dr. Alchurch, Billy Driscoll, and Collin McIntyre remained unharmed.

An unholy anger built within her. She flung dagger after dagger at the objects of her hatred. She might as well have been throwing tissue paper at them for all the effect it had. She spun around to look at the three Angels of Fire. They paid her no heed. She screamed at them to acknowledge her. The Angels stood fast in their place. She hurled her daggers of anger at the Angels. Nothing. There was not a flinch, not a twitch, no sign at all that the Angels were even aware of her presence, though they were quite aware, indeed.

Frustrated, Ora turned her attention back to the hospital and threw at the building all of the hatred and poison she had left.

Inside the hospital all the lights blew in a shower of sparks. Emergency lights flashed in hallways. In operating rooms, backup lighting came on but then went out after a few seconds. In the emergency room, wiring in equipment for monitoring vital signs shorted and caught fire, starting sprinkler systems throughout the hospital.

In the now darkened operating rooms, patients went into cardiac arrest or bled uncontrollably. In a short time, every patient undergoing major surgery had died.

In twenty rooms, elderly patients, dependent on oxygen machines, struggled for breath, as they, too, slowly perished in pain. In only three places was peace to be found: Collin's room, the ICU, and the nursery.

She marveled at her own power and weakness. She wondered at the nature of God. She, an Angel of Hate, could destroy worlds with a thought, but she could not force the Guardian Angels of the doctor, Collin, and Billy to even take notice of her. She couldn't understand how their supposedly loving God protected some and not others. It was these questions, or rather, the lack of answers to these questions, that had spurred Ora down the path she was now on.

In a time before there was time, she and all other Angels, in all their choirs, had been created, and none had been created evil. All creation had the inner Eternal Spark of the One True God. The Angels of Hate had asked questions and had not gotten answers.

This had been the reason for the Great Fall, the battle that had sent them all to hell, hell being the place farthest from heaven.

The answer to these eternal questions was so simple that she could not see it. The Angels, called not only to protect the earthly lives of a few but also to bring home a regiment of holy souls, did not save all the lives in the hospital that day. These lives were instead called to a service that would one day save countless millions. For their lives here, but a fragmentary wisp of the breath of God, were made heavenly martyrs, their prayers amplified ten thousand-fold.

Nevertheless, she had some part of her revenge. The flaming Angels remained unmoved. She marveled one last time and then fell back into the stream of thought and drifted back to her body. On the bench, her eyes opened. The pain was gone, the wounds healed, and her master stood before her.

CHAPTER NEXT

Caleb, dressed in jeans, a green oxford button-down shirt under a green cable-knit cashmere sweater, and cordovan penny loafers, walked happily but purposefully toward his truck, got in, and started the engine.

He always loved the satisfying rattle of the diesel as it fired up. He had had it specially fitted in the truck by some really crazy mechanical geniuses in Boston. Cal had met them while working on a case.

They had helped him as expert witnesses in court, testifying that a human body could, indeed, be chopped up in small enough pieces to be fed into the air intake of a large diesel motor, thereby being combusted and sent out the exhaust as smoke. These guys had tested Caleb's hypothesis using a cadaver from the county morgue. They christened the motor "Death Eater" and installed it in Caleb's truck, much to Cal's delight.

Most criminals were quite stupid, but not all. The diesel engine body-burning guy was brilliant. He was also a homicidal nut who had killed his own mother with a hatchet for burning his toast. Nice guy. Caleb met all kinds in his job.

As he backed out of the driveway, he stopped, got out, and put the top down, because the Fall morning was crisp and cold, with the smell of a woodstove burning last year's oak biting into his nose, and he loved that.

The land adjacent to his property was an apple orchard. He could smell the sweet-sour scent of unpicked apples rotting on the ground and large pots of mulled cider heating in the orchard's kitchens. It was paradisiacal.

This year's Autumn had started quietly enough. The flocks of swallows had been right on time, flying in one unified swarm, left and right, up and down, until, signaled by something forever unknown to us, they landed, all of them at once, on the power lines. The swallows were the sign that Autumn had truly begun.

Cal drove to town, slowly, absentmindedly, watching the brown leaves blow in the wind on the side of the road. He didn't think about where he was going; he just went on autopilot, for two miles.

It had been a year since the tragedy at the hospital. Collin and Billy had put the past year's experiences behind them, as children can sometimes do. Having strong families and close friends had saved them from permanent trauma.

Dr. Alchurch was another story. He was not traumatized, exactly, but the experiences in the woods had changed him. Most days, when not at work or reading, he could be found sitting in his garden in the lotus position, of all things, praying the Rosary.

His comment was, "I am a Zen Catholic now. Thank you, Father Merton."

He now was in Boston with Harry more than he was at his practice. Just as the killing of Asgeir Jorgensen had set Caleb on his life's path, that day in the woods reset Dr. Edgerton Alchurch on his.

The authorities had not determined a definitive reason for the power surge, outage, and fire at the hospital that terrible day. The public was told that a probable faulty unit at the local power substation in conjunction with a very strong solar flare had been the ultimate cause of the problem.

Most accepted the story. Some, always looking for conspiracies, did not. These people came up with some very creative ideas for what had happened that day, ranging from the CIA to the Vatican as being responsible. No one, not even the conspiracy kooks, could have dreamed that the truth was so much stranger than their paranoia-fueled theories. The truth was so much stranger that, even if it had been told, no one would have believed it.

Cal had been consulted about the events at the hospital. He had gained a worldwide below-the-radar reputation as the go-to man for problems that seemed to have an unknown cause and no solution.

Caleb could offer no hard solution for the hospital tragedy to the authorities, but what he could do was ask the right questions, pointing those in charge and himself in the right direction. What he did do—better than anyone else, really—was admit that he didn't know what was going on in a case and then ask beautifully constructed what-if questions. Many blood-soaked puzzles and murders had been solved by Caleb first saying, "I don't know, but…"

During the twelve months since the "hospital incident," as Caleb thought of it, there had been other events of interest to Caleb going on around the world. Almost no one on the planet had taken special notice. What had happened seemed run-of-the-mill tragic to most. It was reported on the news as just another earthquake, just another ten-car pileup, just another fire at some factory in some third-world country no one seemed to care about.

To Caleb Michael Smith, however, some of these incidents stood out. He had kept careful track of these happenings in a marble notebook. He did not like to type these things into his computer. The act of writing with a pencil on paper primed the pump of his brain, somehow. Gemma, who was now his wife, would enter the notebook stuff in the computer at some time in the future.

To check his intuition, he did run all the variables to which he had access through a software algorithm he had written. The software analyzed the variables—sometimes hundreds of them— and predicted with great accuracy what the forces behind a social situation were. The software had backed up Caleb's intuition every single time.

The pattern was becoming too clear to ignore. Just as an asteroid orbiting the sun can have its path traced back through millions of years, even to its own origin, so these events could be traced to one pivotal event in Caleb's own past and from that point to dozens of other points in the past of North Island. It was apparent, too, that the event in his past and the events of the last twelve months were showing him that something big was brewing for North Island and the world.

It was going to happen soon.

MURDER ONE

A teacher, a classic spinster type with horn-rimmed glasses and hair in a tight bun who lived in rooms at the school, always woke well before dawn to prepare the lessons for the day. She had made the horrible discovery and called 911. The lights and the sounds that had awakened the island at 4:00 a.m. were the helicopters of different law-enforcement agencies landing at the school. When you live fifty miles off the coast, calling in the big guns of law enforcement was an event resembling the landing at Omaha Beach. The ferries, the coffee shop, and the grocery had all opened an hour earlier than normal in response to both the need and the excitement of it all.

Caleb was met at the school door by a group of lawmen: the town cop, who was Sheriff Parsons, state troopers, county sheriffs, FBI—all the agencies save for the FBI were represented more to let the public know that there were men here to protect them more than to be truly useful. They all looked at Caleb. His face and presence were both familiar and expected, but their eyes held the horror of what lay above.

He approached the open doors of the building and went through. The old school was just as he remembered. Not much had changed in the twenty or so years since he had been a student. The paint was the same; the ornate woodwork was the same; the smell was the same. It was a school day, but classes were not in session. Parents had been called, and all students sent to their rooms without explanation. The soapstone staircase, paneled on both sides by some ancient oak cut from the woodlands of their island, led to the topmost floor. He made his way up the steps deliberately, one by one, arriving at the top landing reluctantly. From there he walked the few steps to the classroom door and saw the body, if it could be called that, hanging from an electrical cord.

The unholy, sickening sight of it stopped him cold. It was Saint Petersburg all over again. The vision of Fathers Konstantin and Fadeev hanging by their necks in the church flooded his mind. Nausea took hold of him. Caleb turned and took a few steps away from the room. There he stopped, gathered himself, did an about-face, and returned to the entrance of the room. He had seen some gruesome things, but seeing this scene again rattled him to his very soul. Sometimes being a man was almost too hard.

The freshly skeletonized remains swung very slightly in the honeysuckle-scented breeze that came through the open window, swung with a metronomic rhythm and dripped with blood and sinew. The head was crooked to its own left, and the face looked directly at Caleb as if to ask, "Why did you let this happen to me? Why did you not stop this evil before it got me?" The only indication of this wretch's former identity was a Saint Theresa medal hanging from the neck. Caleb stood there, eyes fixed on the ghoul with a lipless smile, dangling from a zip cord.

Caleb averted his eyes and approached the lead investigator, Frank Coughlin, a man he had known for more than twenty years, and cleared his throat to get Frank's attention. The investigator's face was ashen. The victim had been a girl. This much, only, was certain: the bones told the story.

Cal turned to the investigator. In hushed, respectful tones, he said, "Frank, what have your men made of this? People are going to be frightened to death. You read a little about the case I handled in Russia? I have seen this very thing before."

Frank, a man about ten years older than Caleb, of stocky, muscular build, salt-and-pepper hair tightly cut, marine fashion, looked at Caleb with an empty, icy stare. "I know, Cal. I read your reports and descriptions. When I saw this"—he pointed to the victim— "I hesitated to call you, because I knew how affected you still are by Saint Petersburg. I can see now that I should have warned you."

"No, Frank. I am glad that you did not. I might not have come, and I know that I need to be here. I need to solve these cases."

Frank had been through wars in both Iraq and Afghanistan, but this was worse than anything he had seen in those two places. He looked drained. "There's more, I'm sorry to say. You know Paul Smith? Some of his goats and sheep were killed last night, too. We found them hanging by their hind legs, skinned to the bone, just like this girl, hanging by the same kind of cord. Paul is in a real state. What in God's name are we going to do? This is bad. This is very, very bad. We have no clues here. No prints, no blood except for hers, no fibers, no evidence of the weapon, and of course, no witnesses. It's as if this was done by a phantom."

Caleb knew that Frank was not a man given to stating the obvious, but the scene in that room was so gruesome, so terrifying in its blatant in-your-face bloodiness that there could be no better way of saying it. Caleb turned his back on Frank and made for the door, motioning for the investigator to follow him.

When Caleb was outside the room, out of sight of the sickening presence hanging there, he turned to Frank and said with quiet anger in his voice, "I have my ideas about what happened here and I don't think that 'phantom' is terribly far off the mark. But how do you fight someone—something—that leaves no fingerprints, no evidence of itself, of any kind? I've been chasing these damned phantoms, phantoms who seem to carry very sharp knives, for a long time now. I have definitely seen more death in the last week than I had ever hoped to see in my entire life!"

Caleb continued, through gritted teeth and bile rising in his throat, "Damn it, damn it, damn it all to fuck. Do we know who she is? Not that it makes a difference, but it makes a difference. Is she local? Is she someone we know? Is she a student? Who in fucking burning hell is hanging in there?"

Frank, who had been staring at his own shoes, lifted his head and said, "We haven't even talked about her identity among ourselves, but there is a strong feeling that she is Marianne Jorgensen."

His voice broke as he whispered the name, and Cal braced himself against the wall. "So far, she's the only person not accounted for in the student body, and the only girl who might have been here alone at the time we think this happened, because she has a habit of getting up in the middle of the night to study here."

When Cal heard the name, his blood ran cold in his veins. *No, no, no, no, no!* It could not be the Jorgensen girl. This could not be happening twice to the same family! The evil was back. Or maybe it had never left, only slept. The evil had claimed a victim, had quenched its thirst for blood for the first time in more than two decades.

Caleb looked Frank squarely in his steel-gray eyes, gave him the very slightest of acknowledging nods, and returned to the room. Caleb raised the camera to his eye. The camera was like a shield between himself and the skeleton hanging before him. He focused on marks on the right shinbone and pressed the button on top of the camera to capture the images he needed to look at later.

What went through his mind at times like this truly astounded him. He thought, *Digital photography is artificial photography. I hope that Fred's Diner hasn't run out of today's special before I get out of here. Did I return that book to the library?*

He thought these things to protect himself from what he was seeing. He did not want this to be real. The bones in his viewfinder were real enough, though. Fifty photos taken and saved. He was done.

Cal looked over to a county sheriff's deputy, a man of long acquaintance, and said, "Jim, I am done and gone. Will you please tell whoever cares that this poor girl can be cut down now?"

Jim said, "Cal, I am glad to be outta here, too. I've got a daughter, and I can't even imagine…" A tear ran down his cheek. With that, the deputy strode out of the room, leaving Cal alone with the hanging girl for the first time all morning.

The room was almost dead silent. The classroom desks had all been pushed to the walls to make room for the army of men who had been in and out that morning, and Cal, feeling a sudden blast of fatigue, walked over to a desk, sat on top of it, and looked at the girl. "Sweetie, I will not leave you alone here the way you were alone when you were killed. I am going to find out who did this to you, and I am going to get justice for you. I promise you the same promise that I made to Asgeir."

Cal stood up as a team of men, dressed in white suits that reminded him of painter's overalls, came in and took the girl down from her hanging place.

Before he left, Cal told the men, "Guys, please remember that she is someone's daughter." The team, all fathers, did not have to be told. "Jane," short for Jane Doe, was carefully and respectfully taken down and zipped inside a body bag, which was placed on a gurney.

Caleb walked out of the room, crossing himself as he passed Jane's remains. He could not stand to be there any longer but did not want to go home just yet. Gemma was home, with his dogs and he did not want to tell her of this just now; he felt dirty in his mind and soul. His spirit needed to wash off.

Cal walked down the stairs, acknowledging the various men of the teams who had responded but saying nothing. He left the school building, his temples aching and his back somehow hurting. He supposed that he had been holding all the tension of the room in himself, and now it was dissipating.

CHAPTER NEXT

Caleb had been ruminating on what to do. The girl hanging in the school had appeared to him as a recurring nightmare for weeks, not that nightmares bothered him much. However, he had lost more hours of sleep than he could count thinking about this case and had become hardened to staring into space at three in the morning.

He had kept Gemma, his beautiful Gemma, semi-awake with him, her head resting on his shoulder as they sat on the sofa together while he thought. On many of those nights, the girl with the lipless smile spoke to him, imploring him to find her killer. She looked at him with accusing eyes that were not there, shaming him, damning him while hanging before him. In his mind, all he could say back to her was, "I'm working on it."

Caleb had done some of his best, most productive thinking lying in his backyard hammock, and he was tired from lack of sleep, so he walked out his back door and stood on the old concrete stoop, intending to do just that. He was not alone on that stoop, though his companion was unseen and almost unfelt.

Cal had often gotten the sense that, even when he was alone in a room, he was being watched—not spied on but watched over. Right there, standing on the stoop, looking out at the massive trees behind his house, Caleb felt somehow not alone, but he dismissed the feeling as nostalgia. When he was a boy, his mother had taught him that he was protected and loved by his guardian Angel. He noted to himself that whatever he believed regarding his faith, he was a grown man now, and guardian Angels were the stuff of children's bedtime stories.

Caleb's house had been his parents' Summer cottage. They had spent many happy Summers here with cookouts and family reunions, and a few romances had been ignited, caught flame, and burned themselves out in the course of six weeks.

Now he looked out at the woods behind his house and wondered about how scared he had been as a boy looking out on them.

In his mind, he went back to his childhood and remembered hearing voices come from the woods, voices calling to him, calling to him to come into the woods. He remembered the little girl who stood at the edge of those woods with her blank stare from coal-black eyes and her hand outstretched, beckoning him.

The girl spoke to him, although not so much in words. She told him things he did not understand but that left him greatly troubled. She told Cal that she had known him through his ancestors since before time had made itself known on this continent. She came every day for a long time and stood at the edge of the wood, calling to him. Other voices called to him during the night to just come into the darkness of the forest. She was definitely not his guardian Angel.

His other companion, his unseen friend, had a voice, as well, and a name. His name was Michael, or Micha-el. Michael is an Angel of the highest order. Michael is terrible and wonderful. For a human to look directly at Michael would be so quickly fatal that the human would be dead for a week before he knew what had happened to him.

Michael was almost never assigned to be any one person's guardian, but this particular person was special, with a special job to do. So though Caleb was unaware of the presence about him, the voices calling from the trees knew all too well who was standing guard over him.

Would Michael let any real harm come to Caleb? Even Michael did not know what the Father had planned for Caleb. So, if the Father intended for Caleb to die at some point, there would be nothing Michael could do about it. Michael hid himself, now even from the throng in the trees, and the girl, small as she was, saw a chance to act.

Cal looked out into the spaces between the trees and felt as if he could almost see the girl and her throng, seemingly forever trapped there, as if captured in a sylvan cage, waiting for something or someone to let them out.

Cal closed his eyes and felt that odd longing that he had known through so many of the days of his childhood, a longing to run into the forest and hide among the leaves and thickets, to live there and be a part of whatever it was that had called to him for so long. He lost himself in these half thoughts for some minutes. His attention was so engrossed in these thoughts of a final peace that he did not notice that the forest had gone quiet, deadly quiet.

As he stood there, eyes closed, slowly breathing in and out, almost regretting his decision not to run into the woods, he heard from his right a huge cracking sound. He turned just in time to see the girl with the black eyes and the green ribbon in her hair staring at him from behind the now falling beech tree.

The crack of the wood, the sight of the girl, the falling of the tree all happened so fast that he did not have time to move before the trunk of the tree struck him, crushing him beneath its monstrous weight. Cal was flat on his back, bloody and broken, losing the fight to stay conscious. From the sky, coming from nowhere, the last thing he saw before passing out was a green ribbon fluttering down toward his face. The girl looked down on his form with disgust, hissing to herself silently and with deadly intent.

The screen door opened behind Cal's nearly lifeless body, and she was inside the house, looking, searching, hunting. She moved through the house with no sound. In the living room, the two dogs slept the sleep that only the truly innocent can achieve. She hovered over the dogs, and their blood started, ever so slightly, to coagulate in their veins, and their hearts began to struggle. Jacob and Missy woke with labored breathing, frightened, not understanding what was happening to them. She looked down upon the two helpless dogs, cherishing their pain, devouring their panic.

Michael had been present the entire time and was going to let this situation with the dogs go only so far. Michael spread his wings over the two terrified dogs, and their pain was over faster than it had begun.

Michael also stood over the slowly dying dogs, and in a breath, he loosed their blood and restored their hearts. Caleb lay under the trunk of the tree, his body fighting for life and losing the battle.

The girl, confused and seething, focused her hate on the dogs but felt that same hate forced back on herself. Michael looked at her with a holy and sacred anger, and she felt the weight of his anger pressing down upon her.

She choked on her own vile, putrid mind. Gone, then she was gone, crushed into a black hole, falling in on herself, in an infinity of retching death. Then Michael was gone.

"Hello? Hello? I can't see. I can't open my eyes. Is there anyone here?", Caleb choked through blood in his mouth.

"Open your eyes, Caleb," said a voice so deep and masculine that Caleb could feel it rumble through him and shake out into the heavens that he could not see.

Caleb was now able to open his eyes, and he saw a blackness so complete that it gave him vertigo. Slowly, slowly, slowly, as his "eyes" adjusted to this new place, he could see points of light—tiny, but intensely bright—off in the distance in every direction.

He heard the voice again, this time just as deep and rumbling, yet this time carried on a wave of love and understanding for which Caleb did not have the words. The blackness was instantly replaced by overwhelming brightness.

From the formless light the voice continued, "It is not your time, and you must go back. You would not pay attention, so I had to get your attention. Ten thousand pounds of tree seems to have done the trick."

"You have got my undivided attention. OK, am I dead?"

"For now."

"For now?"

"Yes, for now. You must go back. What have you done with your life?"

"Done with my life? Quite a bit, I think."

"You have. However, there is one thing that you *have not done*."

"What is that?"

"It is the one thing that you were supposed to do. The one thing that you have not done."

Then the world exploded. A white-hot fire consumed Caleb and the light and the blackness, and Caleb was back in his body.

The voice commanded him to get up and go into the house. He opened his physical eyes, astonished that he could do even that, and further, that he could breathe easily.

Cal put his hands under the massive tree, and at the same time, great wings beat with a heavenly wind, and Cal lifted the huge trunk off himself as though it were a twig.

He rose to his feet, bewilderment storming in his brain. He looked at the giant pillar of wood that had crushed him and saw the blood in sickening Rorschach patterns staining the bark. Pieces of flesh ripped from his arms and midsection hung like devilish Christmas ornaments from the broken bits of wood, yet he looked at himself and saw that he was unharmed.

He was in no pain, and he was thinking clearly. He heard the voice again: "Go into the house." So he went into the house. Cal walked slowly and silently through the kitchen to the living room.

The two dogs sat there, tails wagging across the maple floor, perhaps looking a little sheepish, as if they had done something wrong. He knelt, and the two dogs rushed at him, knocking him down, licking his face.

Gemma drove up the quiet, tree-lined road where sat the house she now owned with Caleb, humming the tune to "My Favorite Things" to herself, because she could feel the nip in the air, and her mind always jumped ahead to Christmas.

Gemma loved Christmas, and for her, the season started in late October when the leaves really started to turn. As she neared the driveway, she could see a little girl, her blond hair tied up in a green ribbon, walking into the woods behind their house.

The girl, whom Gemma did not recognize from behind, was carrying a stuffed toy dog in her left hand. The little girl got to the edge of the wood and stopped.

Gemma drove up, parked in the drive, turned off the car, and stared at the little girl who stood at the edge of the woods and the yard, the edge of one world and another. The little girl balanced there, knowing that she was standing between this world and emptiness, this world and self.

This girl tilted her head, and she could feel the worlds collide inside—one world sucking in the other, blacking out the light and the life, the good and the love.

She knew that she held it all right inside her head and could kill or not kill it all on a whim. The little girl felt the deepening ache for the taste of souls on her palate and hunger for the death of all more deeply than ever. One hundred thousand years ago, she had killed half a world, the people of this continent and more, but one had survived. Was it one? Was it more? Her mind scrambled itself, a festering sewer of sickness.

No matter who had lived through her first forays into death, she now felt more powerful than ever before, more powerful than her father, her true father, the father of all things rotting and dead, and she knew that she would one day kill him, too.

Gemma sat in the truck with the smell of leather in her nose and the soft sounds of the breeze playing tag with the leaves on the ground and watched the girl turn around slowly. The girl held up the stuffed toy dog.

Gemma was transfixed by the sight and did not even realize that she had not wondered why a girl, a little blond girl, would be standing by the edge of Caleb's wood holding a toy dog that looked exactly like Jacob. As Gemma looked on, the girl put the toy dog to her mouth and tore out a large part of the stomach of the toy. Gemma's trance was broken when she heard the anguished yelps of a dog coming from the girl's direction and saw the toy spilling what looked like real blood over the girl and the ground around her, while the toy wriggled and twitched in a way that animals hit on the road twitch just before they die.

Gemma, horrified and sickened, put her hand on the car door handle, opened it, and hesitantly stepped out onto the driveway. She closed the door and walked toward the girl, whose smiling face was dripping with blood and entrails. Gemma was almost too stunned to speak.

"What are you?" she asked, barely above a whisper. Gemma continued to walk slowly to the backyard. All the while the girl stood, staring through black eyes set in a bloodstained face. When she had gotten far enough into the yard to see the fallen tree, Gemma's breath left her.

She saw the blood spattered on the bark, the flesh, torn and ripped, hanging in Daliesque craziness from the limbs of the tree. The blond girl began to scream in a voice that sounded like flesh being ripped from bones, like life leaving ten thousand bodies. Gemma looked up to the edge of the wood to find that the girl had gone. From behind her, she heard a twig snap. She spun around to see the little blond girl standing before her.

Gemma stared at the girl. "Wh-who-who are you? What are you doing here? Where is my husband?"

The girl's mouth dropped open, and she replied in a voice that was deep, almost masculine. "You know us; we are many; we are legion. Your Christ banished us from the man whom chains could not hold."

Gemma stood there, not making sense of any of it, eyes on the girl. She understood what she was looking at without understanding why.

The girl, mouth agape, pointed toward the trees. "Gemma, come with us into the wood. Come to see our home. He is there; Caleb is there now, waiting for you, watching for you. Come with us now."

Gemma looked away from the girl toward the house, but it was dark. She noticed that there was no noise, no birds, no wind—nothing but ear-pounding silence. The drapes were drawn in the house, and it appeared empty.

"Where is Caleb? What have you done with him?" she yelled at the girl.

The girl said nothing but lifted a bony finger and pointed to the trees.

Gemma asked again, this time even more urgently, "Where is my Caleb? Whose blood is that?"

The girl, who was looking more and more like a small, desiccated corpse, responded, "Caleb is with us. Caleb has been with us always."

Gemma moved toward the girl, but when she reached the spot where the girl stood, the girl was gone.

From behind her, Gemma heard the girl's voice along with what sounded like hundreds of others calling, "You will see us again," and then the girl was gone.

Gemma's head was spinning, and she was about to go into the woods to look for the girl when she heard Jacob's bark and turned to see him bounding in her direction.

CHAPTER NEXT

Jacob and Missy heard the wheels of the Jeep on the driveway, and they jumped off Caleb and scratched at the door to get out. The dogs knew that Gemma was outside and were anxious to get out to see her.

They were dogs, and what had just happened to them was in the past. However, Jacob and Missy would always carry with them a scar, a reminder of what had happened to them so that if Ora came back, they would know who and what she was.

Caleb stood up and looked at himself in the full-length mirror, propped up against a wall, that was still waiting to be hung in their bedroom. He was not hurt. Cal did not really understand why, and his mind reeled at the idea of it. He must be in shock. He should be dead. He had been crushed by a tree big enough to flatten a car, and he had lived. He continued to look in the mirror, shaking his head in disbelief. It was too big and too weird to understand. Maybe it was some sort of hallucination.

Gemma was outside, and the dogs continued scratching at the door to get out. Cal opened it, and the two dogs were out like a shot. He was not quite so fast out the door. Caleb knew what had just happened to him, but he felt distanced from it, somehow. The falling of the tree, his lifting of the tree, the girl—it was all too much to think about now. He just wanted to see Gemma but stood at the doorway not moving. An hour before, he had been standing on the back porch looking out on the trees and thinking deeply about his childhood, wishing he had run away to be with the girl.

In his dreams, when he was a boy, he had run away with the girl many times, but now he felt found and saved and wanted to savor this feeling for a minute. His head was now clear, and so was his heart.

Caleb Michael Smith moved slowly from the top step of the stoop and around the house to see Gemma on one knee, being kissed all over her face by Jacob and Missy. He walked slowly to her, and bending down, he took his wife and the dogs in his arms.

In that instant, he truly realized he should be dead. What he did not know was that a dark, evil, and powerful Angel had tried very hard to kill him, though somewhere, some part of him knew. Another Angel, *the* Angel, Michael, "He Who Is like God," before whom even the mighty Lucifer had fallen, had, without even the slightest effort, stifled the sickly capricious desires of the Black One. Michael had saved Caleb. Michael saved Caleb because of who Caleb was, because of who he is, and because of who he will be.

Cal and Gemma rose, and she stood in the embrace of her man, soaking up his love. She bathed in his manly strength, knowing that, as much as he had to carry, Caleb would always have to the strength to carry her and protect her, too. Gemma knew that her man was special and that, therefore, the war against him, the assault on his psyche, and the forces set to end him would also be special.

This woman, who unbeknownst to her could trace her own lineage back to the biblical Elizabeth herself, did not become

86

frightened of the future. She simply stood with her man, saying only, "I know that you will say nothing, but you can tell me anything."

Cal said nothing, but to himself he thought, *Gem, sweetheart, the game is afoot. Or maybe it never ended. I am not sure. The darkness haunts my dreams. It follows me like a cloud that tries to scramble my thoughts. I feel as if I'm being hunted from within and without.*

The battle was being waged on two fronts: the outer fight against an evil that seemed to have no end, and his struggle to be rid of the fight.

Gemma had known all of this from the time she was a teenager. She had loved and accepted Caleb from day one and had walked into her relationship with him with her eyes wide open. She loved him, and that was that. She was married to him and would stay married to him, because she needed him and loved him dearly. That was enough for her. As usual, like so much in life, there was much more to it than just that.

CHAPTER NEXT

That evening, Caleb fucked Gemma hard and fast, then hard and slow over the course of hours.

While they were still in the backyard, Caleb felt something inside himself click. He felt suffused with new purpose and also a release of strongholds that had held him back for years. He picked her up, threw her over his shoulder, walked into the house, and tossed Gemma on their bed. He towered over her, and she looked up at him through tousled hair, her dress up around her waist.

What's this? Gemma thought. *This isn't my Caleb, but I like it!*

Gemma wondered if Cal was going to have his way with her. His strength and power sent shivers down her spine and tingles between her legs. The look in his eyes told her that he was not to be trifled with, and that further enflamed her desire.

Caleb undid his belt and removed it from the loops in his pants. Gemma's eyes got big, and she gasped ever so slightly. The idea that Cal might use the belt on her made her head swim, and she could feel herself grow ever more wet.

Cal placed the belt on a hook next to the bed, made a mental note that a paddle would look good hanging there, and, facing her once again, removed his underwear. This time Gemma's breath truly left her. She had never seen her husband so hard. The head of his penis was so big and purple that she thought he might explode right there in front of her. She could not take her eyes off it, and when she saw a little bit of precum dripping from the tip, she involuntarily licked her lips. Gemma was truly on fire now.

She decided to test her husband, to resist him and his advances to see just how badly he wanted her.

Caleb seemed to be able to read her mind, because he looked her in the eye with a little smirk and said, "Turn over on your stomach. Now."

Gemma looked back up at her husband and said, "No. Why don't you make me?"

Caleb was a man who, on that very day, had been killed but did not die. On his worst days, he did not let the bone go away with the dog, but the events of that day had changed him in a way he did not yet understand, and he was not about to let the caprice of his wife keep him from taking what was his.

Cal cocked his head a little to the side and demanded, "What did you say to me, little girl?"

"I said, 'Why don't you make me?'" With that she pulled her dress down over her knees in defiance of his order. She could tell by the glint in his eye that the harder she fought him, the harder he might take her, and the more mind-blowing her orgasm would be.

"Honey, you are screwing with the wrong man on the wrong day." He grabbed her ankles, turned her over as if she weighed nothing, hiked her dress up over her hips, pulled down her panties, and smacked her backside.

"Ouch, that hurt! What are you doing? Put my underwear back!" She struggled to turn herself over, but Caleb held her in place.

"Put your ass in the air."

Gemma ignored him. The smack had aroused her even more, and she wondered how far he would take this, but she said, "I hardly felt that."

"You just said ouch."

"Faking."

"So be it." Caleb raised his hand again and brought it down hard on the other cheek. Gemma yelled a little in pain and delight. Cal grabbed one of their pillows and shoved it under her abdomen, raising her bottom to just the right height for easy entry.

Gemma looked over her shoulder. "Caleb Smith, I don't know who you think you are, but if you think—"

Before she could finish her sentence, Caleb had mounted her and put his hand over her mouth. He drew the head of his penis down the crack of her backside.

Gemma, even without Cal's hand covering her mouth, would not have been able to finish speaking. All she could manage was a shudder and a muffled squeak as she felt the heat of her husband's penis against her bottom.

Cal got his position just right and thrust deep into his wife. He filled her with himself, leaned down to her left ear, and asked her, "Did you feel that?" He began thrusting with a power that Gemma had not felt before.

Sweat began to drip from his face and onto her as he continued to fuck her—sometimes fast, sometimes slow, sometimes pulling all the way out to tease her, sometimes ramming himself balls deep and grinding on her for all he was worth.

Just as he was at his peak, he pulled all the way out, stood behind Gemma, turned her over again, pulled her to him, and picked her up. She wrapped her legs around him, and he pinned her to the bedroom wall and entered her again, pounding so hard that he knocked some Hummel figurines off a shelf. Happily, they landed on an overstuffed chair.

Gemma started to say, "Please fuck m—" but Caleb again stopped her, this time by covering her mouth with his. He kissed her deep and hard and wet.

Again, just as he was at climax, Caleb turned, and without removing himself from her body, put her on their bed, fucking her with a ferocity that he would not have allowed himself the day before.

This time, as he approached climax, he did not hold back. He felt semen pour from his penis into his wife. He then collapsed, his full weight on top of her, each soaked with the other's sweat.

Cal rolled over onto his side and pulled his wife close. She put a hand on her husband's face and said, very softly, "I love you."

"I love you, too. OK, put your ass in the air."

This time, Gemma did not argue.

After, as she lay next to Caleb, Gemma, more satisfied than she had ever been in her life, had many things rush across her mind, all of which she kept to herself. One thought in particular kept at her. The fun of the evening had pushed these thoughts from her mind. Now, they came flooding back.

Gemma bit her lip and turned her back to be spooned by Caleb. She tried to sleep but could tell that Caleb was still in no mood for sleep. She turned around to face him, and Cal put her hands on the bed above her head and kissed her lightly, just brushing her lips with his. She looked him in the eyes and saw the most beautiful man she had ever seen. Caleb Michael Smith had always been very handsome to her, but since he had been physically and emotionally inside of her a few moments ago, his blue-green eyes seemed to take on a phosphorescent glow. Cal returned her gaze, pressed her wrists ever so lightly into the mattress, leaned in, and kissed her again, more forcefully this time. His mouth parted hers, and he probed her mouth with his tongue while she happily yielded to him. Cal moved his hands from hers and enveloped Gemma in a warm and passionate embrace and was with her once again. Gemma, feeling her man love her, was lost in a sea of pleasure and love.

An hour later, Gemma again lay against Caleb. Her head rested on his broad chest. The nagging thought came back, patiently knocking on the door to her awareness. Gemma pushed it back, but it returned like a pestering child who would not be ignored.

She opened her eyes and kissed Caleb. "Cal, my darling man, this has been the best afternoon that any woman has ever had. I know that you love me, and I love you. I love you more than you could ever understand. I know that you love me with all of your heart. I want you to know that you will never be alone. You will never have to fight these demons alone. That is a promise. I love you more than the evil hates you."

Cal opened his mouth to protest that he did not need her help. He wanted to say that he was a man, but Gemma quickly put her mouth on his to quiet him. She kissed him with a soft and gentle passion that told him that he was safe with her and always would be.

CHAPTER NEXT

Caleb had been very popular with both boys and girls when he had attended the island's school as a day student. The boys liked him because he was athletic and funny. The girls liked him in a different way, but for the same reasons.

Still, he had been a little bit of a loner when the mood struck him, and he had found a place on the school grounds, an abandoned chapel, where he could be alone with his thoughts and God. In his senior year, he had brought Gemma to this place after their marriage, because no one else, but for the two of them, seemed to go there any longer.

Cal had not been to his secret spot since his last day of high school, when he went just before the big bonfire, but he could find his way there in the dead of night, blindfolded. He walked to the north and around the school building, moving through flower and vegetable gardens maintained by the students and past the greenhouses where seedlings for the school vegetable garden were started.

As Caleb passed the "new" hundred-year-old chapel, he could feel the presence of the Holy Eucharist and silently crossed himself.

The cobbled path ended abruptly, and Cal was walking on dirt and grass. He walked without thinking, looking down the entire way, until he came to a stand of long-needle pines. When Cal reached the center of the stand, he stopped and looked up. The magnificence of the trees, standing around him like columns of a cathedral, their branches the flying buttresses, took his breath away.

On the ground was a brown carpet of needles. The air was scented and still. Cal stood on the spot where he had countless times prayed, among other activities, with the girls of the island.

He sat on his old praying spot and tried to pray. As usual, nothing. Dry as dust. Gemma had the faith; Caleb had the intellect. He lay down, crossed his legs, and stared coldly up at the trees. As he lay there he called out silently to God to help him. God was on radio silence. He wished that God would show him what had made the marks he had observed on the girl's bones. Another thing bothered him: other than the marks on the bones, there was no evidence of how that poor girl had been killed. Though it was certain that she was killed in that classroom.

Suddenly, he was seized by the urge to get up and run out from the trees. He ran as fast as he could to his truck, and when he got there he drove as fast to his house. On the way he realized that he felt clear again. The stain of that image on his mind had been replaced by a need to look at the photos once more. With another look, he hoped to be able to find the killer.

In his home office, Cal opened his laptop and pulled up the photos from the crime scene. When he had been taking the photos, the marks had seemed like nothing special.

But now he had to look at the photos to be certain. They took a few seconds to load—ages in computer time—because the photos were very high resolution. He opened the first one and enlarged it, then again, and again.

The pic showed the marks on the bones of the neck, ribs, forearms, and legs. To anyone not trained, the marks were just marks.

To an amateur, the marks could be from a knife, a shovel, or anything else hard and sharp. Seen by a real pro in this magnified detail, however, the marks were unmistakably created by teeth and claws and a very hard bladed knife. It could be no other thing. Around him in his office, the glow of screens from computers and TVs gave the room a bluish hue. The red from blood on bone stood out, and Cal felt deep in his gut just how terrifying this attack must have been. The pattern of tooth and claw marks matched nothing in his vast, encyclopedic mind; they matched no animal that he knew of. He sat back in his chair, contemplating what he was looking at on his screens. He turned and picked up a phone on his desk, punching numbers on the keypad deliberately.

In a lab in Boston a man picked up his phone and said, "Caleb Michael Smith, as I live and breathe. What can I do for you, old man?"

"You will be getting a body today. Well, not really a body, but you will see when she arrives."

"She?"

"Yes, Harry, 'she.' I don't want to say too much, but she will be arriving in town very soon via high-speed ferry."

"What don't you want to say?"

"I don't want to prejudice you at this point, but I have an idea about how this girl was killed, and I want to see if you come up with the same idea. It is not pretty, obviously. It never is. It's just that this is more gruesome than most even you have seen."

Harry thought that he had seen it all. Cal had seen the same things, and if Cal thought that this case was somehow worse, it must be bad. Harry was silent for a couple of seconds on the phone, trying to tamp down feelings of excitement that most people would have found inappropriate, and then said, "OK, Cal. You've not steered me wrong yet. I'll get on it as soon as she arrives, and you'll hear from me today. Out."

"You can't fool me with your nonchalance. You're practically giddy about this. Over and out," Cal said with a small laugh. Now was the first time he had felt any kind of relief from the gloom of the day's events, the relief of knowing that the best man in the country was working with him now.

Cal stood up to stretch out his tense back, turned off all the computer screens, sat down again in his swivel chair, and fell asleep.

CHAPTER NEXT

The phone was ringing rather loudly. Caleb was still sleeping in his swivel chair and had been dreaming of his wife, Gemma. He loved her so very, very much.

Cal reached out and grabbed the old-fashioned phone off the hook. "Hello?" he said with a little frog in his throat.

"Cal, it's Harry. How ya doin', old man?"

Cal said into the handset, "Harry, you work in a forensic lab, one of the best and the busiest in the country. How is it that you always sound so damned chipper on the phone?"

"Well, old man, I truly love my work, especially when I have some important news! My findings are preliminary but exciting."

"Important news?" said Cal back into the phone. "Let me point out, again, that you work in a forensics lab. What news would not be important? All right, all right, forget that. What have you got for me?"

Harry said, "You were not kidding when you told me this was a gruesome case. If you can believe it, the situation is worse than it looks."

Caleb shook his head in disbelief. "How in all of God's creation could it be worse than it looks? She's a teenage girl, gutted to the bone and hung by a lamp cord from a rafter in a boarding school."

Harry was almost bubbly in his reply. "Cal, old friend, it gets worse. Lots worse. Those marks were made by teeth. Well, not all of them were made by teeth. The deepest of the cuts were made by a very sharp knife. There are microscopic fragments of the blade material in her bones. Like no other material I've ever seen. But, we'll see."

Cal interrupted. "The teeth part I figured out. I just wanted you to come to that conclusion on your own."

"Ha!" Harry shouted into the phone. "But that's not all! There's more! Can you believe it?"

Cal could believe it. If he had not actually seen everything, he could, at this point in his life, believe anything.

"Oh, yeah, Cal, old man, there's more. The teeth that made these marks are not human."

"Then what in the world are they?"

"Those marks that were not made by a knife were made by a wolf or wolves."

Cal felt that familiar ache in his temples. Where, oh where was the hard science, the cool beauty of numbers, the wonderful, icy logic that cut through all this mystical mumbo jumbo?

"Harry, I can believe it, but I would rather not. OK, the teeth that made the marks are from a wolf. That is more than disturbing. Somehow I sense that there's more, Harry. You sound too excited."

Harry sounded like he was about to achieve climax, and maybe he already had. Cal had stopped trying to figure out his friend a long time before this.

"OK, Harry. You're having me on. I get it. Now what really made those marks?"

"I'm telling you, Cal, the teeth marks were made by a wolf."

"Harry, what you're telling me sounds impossibly stupid."

"Look, some of the marks are cuts made by a knife, a very sharp knife. I can tell by examining the sample under the scanning electron microscope. A very tiny piece of the blade chipped off in the well of her pelvis, and we analyzed the metal. From that analysis, we could trace the knife to a type found in Jerusalem during Biblical times. However, some of the marks were absolutely made by a very large wolf."

"But how do you really know?"

"For one thing, Cal, I found a wolf tooth embedded in the cartilage in her left knee."

CHAPTER NEXT

The next morning Caleb lay in bed, awake in the dark room, his head and Gemma's on her homemade pillows beneath the open window. On a nightstand, next to the bed, was the camera that had taken the terrible portraits in blood the day before. A slight wisp of a breeze pushed through the screen, softly washing over the man and woman in the bed. He was on his back, taking in the outside air faint with the smell of hickory smoke.

George Miller must be smoking venison; I should remember to buy some, he thought.

Gemma was still sleeping because it was early, and because lying there she felt secure and safe in his arms. He felt secure because she was in his arms. The scent of her hair mixed with the hickory in the breeze threw warm shivers down his spine, and he held her all the closer to himself.

Cal was awake because the first ferry from the mainland would arrive in less than an hour, and he wanted to be there to meet it. The Jorgensen girl was still missing, and no positive ID had been made on the remains found hanging in the school; her DNA was not in any database. Other than DNA, the full results of Harry's analysis were due back on the first ferry. There was no way that Cal was going to trust this type information to either snail mail or e-mail.

As he lay there, Cal felt Gemma's warm skin against his. He held her with his left arm as his right hand caressed her from shoulder to hand, and she woke with a small, girlish sigh.

"Gemma, love, I have to get dressed and go to the ferry slip." She looked up at him and pulled the comforter up to her chin.

"Please don't go. Please!" she said. "I don't want to be alone, and besides, I am having one of my 'feelings.' You know, when I feel that something bad is going to happen. I'm scared, Caleb!"

He put his hand on her face, kissed her forehead. "Don't worry, babe; Jacob will bark if anyone comes near the door, and then Missy will eat them. Besides, I'll be only half an hour or so."

"Half an hour is long enough," she said with a shudder.

CHAPTER NEXT

Gemma lay in the bed that still smelled of her man, her hard-won man, snuggling Jacob and hearing Caleb in the living room say to Missy, "Go on, girl, go protect Mama and Jake." Though Missy was no bigger than Jake, her bite was much worse than her bark. Then Gemma heard the door slam behind him.

Missy came bounding into the room and, with a single leap, was up on the bed, licking Gemma's face. Gemma held Jacob close to her, and Missy settled in next to her on Caleb's side of the bed, which made both Gemma and Missy feel more secure.

"Jake, you'd better bark loudly if you hear anything; it's still dark out, and Mama is a little afraid," she said, giving him a smooch on his snout. Soon the trio was sleeping again. Gemma fell into one of those slumbers that seem to happen only in the early morning, a sleep that feels deep and delicious and feels equally terrible when it is taken away suddenly. Jacob, always on the job, was the first to detect that all was not right. He opened his eyes, and his little tail started to whir, waking Missy. She nudged her nose under Gemma's arm.

Gemma came to semi-consciousness and said, "Not now, Missy. I'll get breakfast when Papa gets back home." She started to go back to sleep. There was a knock at the door.

Gemma thought, *Cal, my dearest, how did you manage to lock yourself out of the house when we never lock the door?*

She got out of bed, still groggy, padded to the front door, and opened it. There was no one there. Gemma stepped back, a little scared. She remembered that some kids had been playing pranks on all the houses lately. Nothing serious, just some TP and the old 'knock and run' but not this early in the morning. Gemma made her way back to bed, snuggled in next to Jacob and Missy, and began to doze off, still eagerly anticipating the return of her man.

The Dark Angel who had hovered over the island like a cloud of poisonous hate had also waited for Caleb to leave the house and knew that it was time to bring a little bit of hell to Gemma before he returned.

In the adjacent room, a book fell from the bookcase, landing on the floor with a loud thud. Startled, Gemma woke and yelled in fright. In a shot, Missy was off the bed. Gemma threw off the covers, picked up Jacob and placed him on the floor, and slowly made her way to the next room. On the floor was a copy of the Bible open to the Apocalypse of Saint John the Apostle. On the desk below the bookshelf from where the Bible had come, the screen for Caleb's PC was on.

Gemma stood there staring at the screen and started to openly weep when she read the words scrolling across it: "What if he never makes it home? We shall not lose, this time."

She fell to the floor next to the Bible, with Missy and Jacob licking her face and her right hand in doggy worry and concern for their mama. Gemma cried and shook and felt sick to her stomach. Missy started to bark loudly at the door, and Caleb came rushing in, breathless.

He saw Gemma on the floor, crying, and dashed to pick her up. "What's the matter, babe? Why are you crying?" Then he saw the big LCD computer screen. It read, "She's dead already." He reached for the off button on the monitor to shut it off before Gemma could look up and see it again, but before he could get to it, those words went away, replaced for just a second with the words "Good-bye, dead man," and the screen went black. Caleb's face took on the look of a man possessed—not by any demon, but of new purpose and determined anger.

He bent over, picked Gemma up in a cradle carry, and took her to the sofa, kissing the top of her head as he walked. He gently placed Gemma on it and kissed her forehead.

He called Jacob and Missy, who came running. Missy jumped up beside Gemma, and Jacob stood against Cal's legs to be hoisted. He placed Jake next to Gemma and Missy, and Gemma hugged them both close.

Caleb said to Gemma, "I'll be right back."

Gemma cried, "No, please don't go! The monitor said that you were going to die!"

"No, I'm not. I am just going over to the coffee maker for a second."

He walked briskly to the monitor and hit the on button. Nothing. The monitor did nothing. From that day forward, it never worked again. Weeks later Cal brought it to some of his electronics pals at MIT, and they analyzed the thing to within an inch of their lives, but not one thing could be found wrong with the device. It just would not work.

Cal returned to Gemma and said, "Gem, this is not like you. Please tell me exactly what you saw that made you fall to the floor."

"I was in bed, with the pups, just as you left me, when I heard a knock at the door. I answered it, but there was no one there. I was a little scared, but I figured it was kids." She sniffled. "The dogs got all agitated, and I went out to see what it was. Your grandfather's Bible was on the floor open to the Apocalypse, and the monitor was on. It said, 'He will never make it home.' I was half-asleep and already nervous about being alone. With you being gone and the knock on the door, it just hit me—maybe you wouldn't come home—and I got so scared."

Caleb thought for a moment. "OK, honey, I'm here now. No worries. It's safe. Don't think about what you saw. I will never leave you. Now, we do have some good news."

"Good news?" Gemma asked, timidly.

"It is actually very good news, and I've got some very good coffee. I hope it will make you feel better." Cal nonchalantly scooped the aromatic coffee into the filter basket, deliberately trying to make the last few minutes seem not so important.

Gemma looked at Jacob while he lay between her knees. Jacob looked back at Gemma and gave her one of those doggy head tilts, as if to say, "I dunno about you, but I want to see if he brought back some very good doggy treats. Let's go!"

After a few moments, Gemma could smell the coffee brewing. With red, tear-stained eyes, though she was still shaken, she said, "Boy, that does smell like good coffee. Should we go, pups?"

In the kitchen, she heard Cal say, "Yes!" Gemma still felt queasy inside, but the sound of Caleb's deep voice had calmed her a little. She got up, set Jake on the floor, motioned to Missy, and said, "One, two, three."

Missy ran ahead into the kitchen, where she found that Papa had indeed brought home some very good treats. Gemma walked gingerly through the living room, peering cautiously at the offending computer screen. This time it was blank and remained that way.

"Listen," Caleb said. "I want you to forget what you saw on that damned screen. It means nothing. The message is just meant to scare us."

"It's doing a good job."

Caleb looked lovingly at his wife and said, "The good news is that the poor girl hanging in the school was not the Jorgensen girl."

Gemma, having seated herself across from Caleb, let out a happy hooray and then caught herself. "But there was some girl hanging there, and her parents, or any relatives she might have, are still wondering where she is." A tear ran down her cheek, and she prayed a silent Hail Mary for the girl and her family. "So where was Marianne?" Gemma asked quietly.

Caleb looked up at her while pouring the coffee and said, "On a ferry to Boston, playing hooky with some mainland girlfriends who convinced her that she ought to have a day of shopping. She's still there, getting ready to catch the next ferry home and catch hell when she gets here."

"You've got to watch out for those mainland girls," Gemma said with a smile.

"Yup," Cal said.

"Her parents are over the moon and fit to be tied at the same time. I think she will be on bread-and-water rations until she is old enough to vote."

"After what her parents went through with Asgeir, I do not blame them one bit," Gemma said. "It may not be fair, and it may not be her fault, but that girl owes some serious amends to her parents."

"It is doubly unfair," said Caleb, "because she has to live in the long shadow still cast by Asgeir. She never met her older brother, and yet she has been made to feel, in an unconscious way by nearly everyone, that she has some big shoes to fill, that she is the last hope of her parents to have a family and the only person who can fulfill her older brother's snuffed-out promise. She may have some more responsibility than other kids her age, but the weight that kid is carrying around is crushing."

"His promise was never really snuffed out. I can feel it. I've been praying on it for years. I have it on good authority that he's been working hard."

Caleb had learned years before that when his wife said such things, to pursue the topic any further would result only in a pain in his temples, so he smiled and let it go.

The dogs happily chewed on new rawhide toys while the first hint of the sun peered through the windows, lifting the gloom and scattering the mystery of the night. Neither Caleb nor Gemma knew how tightly they had been holding on to their emotions until they saw the sun, and then both, without making a noise, let out their breaths and relaxed.

Cal stood at the counter, drinking his coffee and looking over at Gemma. He saw her beauty with a new clarity. Her skin was smooth and flawless. Her face, round and open, had an inviting smile that made him feel at home. She was the most beautiful woman he had ever seen. Her lips were full and soft. Her hands were feminine and delicate, and when they held his hand between them he felt their womanly warmth and love. She was soft and curvy, with short yet shapely legs that made him crazy.

Gemma held her coffee cup to her lips, her long hair creating a sort of veil, and smiled the tiniest of smiles, knowing that Caleb was looking at her. He was looking at her, she could tell, with awe and gratitude. Gemma was still shaken, so Caleb's attention brought forth more tears. Somehow, she knew that she would never lose him, but the thought of it still hurt.

Cal poured another cup. "Another for you, Gem?"

She bit her lower lip in a girlish manner that she knew Caleb would not miss and said, "Sure," as she slid her cup across the countertop. "My forte is prayer. I'm good at it, but fighting this sort of stuff, like I saw on the computer screen…" Her voice echoed with the smallest quiver. "Fighting evil directly is definitely your thing."

Cal breathed a tired sigh. "Yeah, I suppose it is, though sometimes I wish it were not. My prayer life is dry as sand. I try. Nothing. My mind goes blank. I can understand string theory, but I cannot even say 'Hey, howya doin'?' to God. It's been like that for a long, long time."

"I know that, my love. That's why I've been praying for you since we were children. That's why Josh and Patty and your parents pray for you. You're all in your head. You have heart, but you've lost it, lost it in plain sight."

Hearing this, the truth, scared him a little, so he changed the subject. "Listen. How did you ever put up with waiting for me? Why did you wait for me while I was running around with coeds in Boston? I am eternally grateful that you did, but why?"

"I didn't wait, exactly," Gemma replied, looking at him with a love that went past anything else Cal had known before.

"What do you mean? Were there other men before me? I mean, I wanted to go out with your sister when we were kids…."

She cut him off. "No, of course there were no other men before you. As for 'wanting to go out with my sister,' as you so diplomatically phrased it, that's a reason to feel sorry for you and a reason to pray for you and nothing else, as far as I'm concerned. Thank God for Harry. If not for him, you might have gotten your wish. Harry is a better friend than you may ever know. I still don't how he pulled it off."

"Pulled what off?"

"Skip it for now, my dear man. I'll just say that Harry has connections."

"I have an IQ that reads like a zip code, and I do not understand so much of what you say, Gem."

"My dear confused man. The things you don't understand cannot be figured out with a big brain. You must use your heart. If you looked at God the way you look at me and the pups, you would understand instantly. Everything is about God. Always God."

"I know that, Gem."

"Caleb Smith, it's not about knowing, and you *know* that."

Cal could feel his temples aching, again. "The bottom line is this: Marianne Jorgensen is alive; another poor girl, whoever she is, is dead; we have no idea, really, who killed her—or anything about her."

"Caleb, honey, I don't think that this is a case you're going to figure out with your head, at least not all of it. You need to learn to pray. He has your answers, and not just about this case."

Cal's temples pounded all the more. "I'm sunk, then."

CHAPTER NEXT

There are men and women in monasteries who do almost nothing else but work and pray, pray and work. It has been said of these religious monastics that the world would be much better served if they left their cloisters, went out into the world, and performed some good work or otherwise were of direct service to others. What these critics do not see, do not understand, and could never understand, is that, without the Eucharist and the constant intercessory prayer of these ecclesiastical warriors, our world would soon be a dead husk, blown away like so much dust in an evil, heartless wind.

A direction in life is hard to come by for many. People do this and do that, falling into something by default or taking the path of least resistance. And when they die, or are about to, they realize that they have lived the life of a cipher, a cog, easily replaced by the next cog to come along; they have made no difference to themselves or anyone else.

The brothers Caleb Michael and Joshua Payne Smith did not suffer from this problem. They were both intensely focused young men. From the outside, their vocations looked very different, but to anyone who truly knew them, their mother and father, for example, the life choices they made were each a reflection of the other.

Joshua saw evil in the world and knew what he had to do to combat it. Joshua, always the more introverted of the two, chose a life of ascetic monasticism and prayer in the Order of Cistercians of the Strict Observance. Here, he prayed and worked. In so doing, Father Joshua fought a battle "as mighty and important as any man who lived out in the world", as he put it often.

For Caleb, staying home was what he wanted, and home was New England. New England was very important to Cal for a variety of reasons. Yes, it was his home, but not just where he lived. It was part of him, and he part of it. It was as if he had been dug from the warm and fertile earth of New England by the hand of God Himself and fashioned into Caleb Michael Alexander Smith. He was forever connected to the earth that made up his home.

Caleb saw evil in the world as well, and he, too, knew what to do to combat it. He went to college. He wanted to learn everything about everything. Because Cal was a New England boy, a real downeastah, he limited his choice of colleges to those in New England.

While in school, Cal studied Latin and history—American history and the history of the West. He wanted to know all that he could about what had made his world what it was. He graduated in two years, which meant that he was eighteen when he started graduate school, studying electrical and bioengineering and communications physiology. He obtained his PhD two years after that. People with Cal's education background have influenced fields like cognitive science, artificial intelligence, and neural and computer networks. He was intensely focused on the battling of evil in the world directly and had been since the day Asgeir Jorgensen had been killed.

Every day he read the papers, perused the Internet, saw what was going on in the world, and sensed a pattern. He did not yet know what the pattern meant, but he could tell it was there. What he did know was that he was still angry and frightened about what had happened to his little island when he was sixteen.

Given his near obsession with the dark news of the day, and with no concrete ideas about what to do, he did what anyone else would do, and he rented a little storefront office in Cambridge and hung out a shingle that read "Caleb Michael Smith, Consulting Detective." He thought that this was terribly funny, but only a few got the joke. He was disappointed by that.

His first case was brought to him by a relative in the Boston PD. A woman had been raped and murdered, and her body had been left, beaten, bloody, and nearly decapitated, on the steps of city hall. Such a crime had never been seen before, and the police, after months of investigation, were still baffled. Save for the body, there were no clues of any kind. Forensic evidence, forget about it.

Because their best detectives could make nothing out of the case, the BPD made a call to an unknown kid, partly because his uncle, a cop on the force, put a bug in ear of some brass, and they asked him to try his hand at the case. After three weeks of careful examination of what little evidence there was and a lot of sleepless hours ruminating over what all the facts might mean, he thought that he had an answer. None of the pieces of the puzzle fit to make a coherent picture of the events, and so Caleb realized that they were not supposed to. After pages and pages of calculation, he told the BPD that there was an 89.97 percent chance that the murder had been a decoy committed by drug lords and gunrunners.

The BPD, with no other leads, took his information. They found that the killing had been a ruse, a red herring to throw the police off the scent of other criminal activity. The woman was picked at random. She had been the unfortunate victim of drug lords looking to establish a foothold in the Boston area.

If this had been Caleb's only contribution to the case, his name would have been made, but there was more. Cal was able to use his knowledge and education to come up with a computer algorithm for predicting the outcome of events given certain sets of data. When the relevant data points for the rape case were entered into the algorithm, the computer spit out a description of a woman who could have been the twin of the victim.

His career was made, and Caleb was on his path. If he had known where that path would lead, he might have turned back and run very far in the other direction.

CHAPTER NEXT

Mary Colvin Smith, one month into her third pregnancy, her second miracle pregnancy, and a completely unexpected one at that, sat on the large leather sofa, legs curled beneath her, bathed in the soft glow of firelight and gas lamp, humming a tune softly to herself while her long, graceful fingers pulled a needle and thread through fabric held in a maple frame. Artie, her husband, sat to her left, absentmindedly rubbing her stocking-clad foot with his right hand while he read a technical journal on the strength of materials. Mary called this sort of journal her husband's "light reading," always with a playful laugh.

Cal and Josh, eleven and twelve years old, sat in opposite corners of the room, each one hidden behind an overstuffed chair, each one wrapped in a heavy woolen reproduction Navajo blanket, each one reading about cowboys, Indians, and space aliens, feeling safe in the little cocoon of their family. To complete the picture, Artie's own father was in the home's basement woodshop making furniture for clients in Maine. The room in which they sat was the creation of Artie Smith, with some limited input from his wife.

Mary Smith had designed the rest of the house herself to suit a young and growing family and to make it like the house she had dreamed of as a girl, but this room was Artie's own. It looked like something born first in the mind of Normal Rockwell, as it was illuminated, most of the time, solely by gaslight lanterns that gave the whole space a warm hunting-cabin sort of glow.

The room vaulted up twenty feet and was paneled on two sides in age-darkened oak. Some of the hand-hewn beams and all the paneling had been in Artie's grandfather's house, the ruins of which stood only a few miles away. The other two walls were floor-to-ceiling windows, with oak mullions stained to exactly match the paneling. The windows looked out over bluffs covered, on this day, in windblown snow and small native bushes that clung to the bluffs with all their tiny might. The tough little bushes always inspired Artie to never give up in anything.

Even though the windows were specially designed to insulate against the cold, a good deal of the time heavy curtains were drawn to help keep the warmth in and the cold out. Today, however, the curtains were pulled back to reveal a scene of raging tranquility.

The wind blew hard and fiercely, picking up large handfuls of helpless snowflakes, thrashing them this way and that against the windows and the rocks on the bluffs. As violent as the pounding wind seemed to be, the little flakes, with crystalline arms outstretched, caught the wind's grasp and laughed with delicate glee as they careered about, only to settle to the ground to clamor for another ride into the air.

In the cocoon of their room, they sat reading, thinking, and listening to the wind run headlong up the cliffs, listening to the crackle of orange and yellow flames slowly consuming the logs in the stone hearth. It was into this safe and loving haven that evil broke in, ever looking to destroy what it could not have.

The phone on the end table next to Mary Smith rang. It rang with a sort of intensity that should not sound any different from a normal ring but, somehow, does.

Mary picked up on the second ring. From the other end came wailing sobs, sobs that would be echoed five years in the future. She stood up from the sofa and said in a panicked voice, "Gianna, honey, please slow down!"

The frantic voice on the other end was crying and weeping in Italian, and Mary could not get her to slow down, so Mary switched to Italian herself. She said, in the Roman dialect spoken by Gianna, "Gianna, my darling, please. What's the matter? Please tell me what's going on."

Upon hearing her closest friend and confidant speak to her in the tongue of her childhood, Gianna was able to just get out, in English, "Mary, please come, come get me and Gemma now! Please!"

Artie, whose command of languages was even better than his wife's, did not have to be told what was happening. He was already up, retrieving his overcoat and Mary's woolen coat.

Mary spoke, "Artie, honey, maybe I—" and Artie Smith's hand went up, hushing his wife.

Artie went into another room in the house, opened the door to the cellar, and yelled down, "Hey, Pop, Mary and I have some business to take care of. The boys are in the study. Can you just keep an ear peeled for them?"

Artie did not tell his own father where he and his wife were going, because he knew the older man would want to come, and he needed to do this job alone. He also needed someone who could watch the brothers and who had the power to keep them safe should something unfriendly make itself known here.

August Smith came up the stairs and walked with his son to the study. Artie looked at his wife, holding out his hand for her to take. The look in Artie's eyes was one Mary Smith had not seen before. August Smith knew the look but did not say a word.

"Well, boys, it looks like just the three of us for a while. Let's go down to the shop and you can practice your joinery until your old dad and your mom get back."

The boys jumped up and eagerly followed their grandfather to the basement.

Artie's eyes were stone, and his jaw was set in a way that gave his whole face the look of a man who was not going to put up with questions or arguments, so Mary hushed and let Artie help her on with her coat.

He led her outside in the cold and blowing wind, which had become very much more intense in the last ten minutes. Artie opened the passenger door of the International Harvester 4×4 and closed it behind her after making sure that her hands and feet were clear. Other men might have been in a frenzy, rushed, and made more of a mess of things.

Artie Smith never rushed. He was meticulous and methodical, and, at this moment, he was feeling very methodical.

Once in the car, Mary said, "Artie, honey, please go as fast as you can. I am so worried for Gianna! She would not tell me what was wrong, but it must involve her husband."

Artie did not respond. He was a typical male in that he understood what his wife had said, he had acknowledged it in his mind and even agreed with what she said, but he did not see the need for a response.

Mary spoke up. "Arthur Smith, I was talking to you. When I speak to you, I do not want you to ignore me."

Artie looked over at his beautiful wife as he drove the icy road and said, "I'm sorry, sweetheart. Yes, it certainly does have something to do with that scumbag."

Normally, Mary would have told her husband in no uncertain terms that he was to never speak like that in front of her; he needed to have respect. But on this occasion, her response nearly made Artie drive off the road. "That man is a scumbag. That is the perfect word for him."

Artie said not another word for the rest of the drive, thinking only of what he was going to do when he and his wife got to Gianna's house.

Mary finally piped up, "There it is, on the right. The one with no Christmas lights."

Artie slowed down and pulled into the driveway. Mary did not wait for the truck to come to a complete stop but jumped out of the moving vehicle and ran for the front door. This got Artie very upset, because he knew what Gianna's husband was capable of.

Artie caught up to her just as the front door opened. The man sneered. "Well, well. The cavalry has arrived."

The man at the door and Artie Smith were a study in contrasts. Gianna's husband was impeccably good-looking. He had aquiline features, slicked-back jet-black hair, eyes the color of coal, and permanent five o'clock shadow. His clothes always seemed to hang on him perfectly, and his shirttails did not pull out of his pants if he reached up above his head for something. He smiled rarely, and when he did, the person being smiled at generally felt a sick feeling in the pit of his stomach, as if he had just seen a fin rise out of the water between himself and the shore.

Artie Smith was anything but "pretty." He was not sloppy or messy, but neither was he a neat freak. His shirttails, which were always flannel, were almost never tucked in. One short ride in his truck would have them half out anyway, and he would just swear under his breath and pull them out all the way.

His features, far from being aquiline, were ruggedly handsome, and like all the men his family, he had piercing green-blue eyes that seemed to change hue slightly as the day wore on. He was just under six feet tall but gave the impression of being taller. His arms were long for his height and attached to shoulders that looked like canned hams, especially in a T-shirt. He did not wear a watch, as he never felt the need to know the time.

Artie strode up behind his wife. Mary was attempting to reason with the man at the door, trying to get him to let her in the house. Gianna's weeping could be heard faintly from another part of the house, and Mary was beginning to cry. The man had been expecting this, had been expecting Mary to cry and Artie to try to bust into the place like some sort of saving knight. The man at the door had never had any respect for Artie Smith. Artie looked strong physically, but he saw Artie as a soft, churchgoing pussy who was too doting with his children and too lenient with his wife.

In history, there have been some tremendous miscalculations. The Japanese bombed Pearl Harbor thinking that it would some-how cow the Americans into submission. The Japanese were wrong. Saddam Hussein told the world that he would destroy American forces only to see his army itself destroyed within a matter of hours. Napoleon at Waterloo and Custer at Little Big Horn also come to mind. This man's assessment of Artie as a pussy was a slightly smaller mistake than Saddam's, but only slightly.

As Artie appeared behind his wife, the man stopped talking and gave Artie a self-satisfied little smirk. "Mr. Smith," he began. "Sending your wife in ahead of you, I see."

From the unknown part of the house, Artie and Mary continued to hear the sobbing.

The man said, "It doesn't matter which one of you two came first. You can both turn around and take your overly pious, do-gooding selves away from here. We can deal with our own problems. Good-bye."

The man tried to close the door in Mary's face but was stopped by the broad, strong hand of Artie Smith. The man sized up Artie. He had dispatched men quite a bit larger than this. Mary and Gianna had been friends for years, but the man had never spent much time in Artie's company, and so he had never gotten to know Artie. It was for this reason that the man was about to make the worst mistake in judgment of his life. The man, seeing Artie block his closing of the door, stopped and looked at Artie with contempt.

Mary became frightened and ran straight past him, following the sobbing until she found Gianna, looking beaten and bruised, her breathing labored and painful, hiding in a closet with her daughter, Gemma, in her arms. Mary bent down, taking both Gianna and the girl in her arms, and the three of them cried and cried.

Mary said, "Come, Gi, please. Let's get you out of this closet. Gemma, honey, take my hand; we're getting out of here." Finally, from the front of the house, the women heard men fighting, and they saw a small figurine fall from a shelf in the closet as the wall shook from someone being thrown against it.

Gianna cried all the louder. "Mary, my husband is going to kill your Artie! Please! He's going to kill your Artie."

Now, Mary had never seen a certain aspect of her husband. In fact, there were some parts of himself that Artie Smith had always kept a secret, not so much for secrecy's sake but because he just never saw the need to reveal those parts of himself to his wife, his children, or anyone else save his father who had similar gifts.

Even though Mary had never seen these facets of her husband, she knew that she was married to a man whose surface ran a mile deep; there was so much more to him than she knew about. This had always intrigued her and had brought from her respect, for reasons she could not articulate. So, when Gianna started to cry about Artie being killed by her husband, Mary knew somewhere deep in her soul that Artie would be able to handle things and that he would be all right.

From behind Gianna came a shadow, and on seeing this shadow on the wall, she began to scream in terror, "No, no, no! Please leave us alone. No more. I will do whatever you want! Just stop, *please.*"

The shadow bent over, and Artie Smith's square hand rested on Gianna's shoulder, and he said, "Gianna, you will never have to worry about your husband hitting you or your girl ever again. C'mon, let's get the hell out of here."

CHAPTER NEXT

The day before had been another long and exhausting one for Cal; On the phone with investigators in Boston, getting calls from police departments from across the country and around the world. The murders that centered on North Island were not his only cases. At any time, there might be half a dozen cases, ranging from crimes of passion to kidnapping to serial killers plying their trade, simmering away on the burners of his mind.

Lying in bed, spooning his wife, Caleb took a long time to fall asleep. When he finally did, he found himself in a dream, yet awake, standing in a room watching many people. There were tens of thousands of people in the room, all looking at him with one soulless stare. One of them, a devil with no hair and no face—save for a mouth with a broad, toothless smile—walked over to Caleb and handed him a knife. The knife was unusually heavy for its size and had a dark wood handle. Other than that, the blade was nondescript.

The faceless figure stood there smiling at him; it turned and pointed at the now uncountable numbers standing behind him.

The faceless now had faces: the faces of Jews and Gypsies and others killed in Nazi death camps; the faces of crucified Armenians of the twentieth century next to crucified Christians of the first; African slaves, chained in the holds of ships; Native Americans, slaughtered by the thousands, and their white victims on whom they took their revenge. The crowd was in the room with Cal and the faceless, smiling devil and the crowd continued into the distance, and Caleb could see no end to it.

The devil turned once again to face Caleb. From the vast infinities into which the crowds of dead and dying receded, Caleb felt, more than heard at first, a rhythmic beat, a pulse come at him in nauseating waves. The smiling devil began to move in time with the beat. Behind him the throng moved to the beat in perfect unison. The dance looked like a ritualistic offering to a god whose very life came from the suffering and death of those forced to dance and move with him. They moved and sang their unwilling praises to this god of blood.

The faceless man said one thing to Caleb and then vanished. "Look at the bones again."

CHAPTER NEXT

The bones were in Boston, so Caleb, out and about, went home and had his wife pack a bag.

"I don't want you to go, Caleb."

"I know, sweetheart, but I have to. This case may depend on it. I really have to."

"But I get so scared when you're gone. I feel so alone. I won't be able to sleep."

"Honey, I have asked Patty to come stay with you and the pups. Besides, she just got her own dog, a little beagle. She has wanted to bring him over to meet Jacob and Missy. You won't be alone."

A knock and a bark were heard at the door. Before Caleb could get up to answer it, Patty came bounding in with Barney, her little beagle.

Hugs and kisses all around, and then Cal said, "See, sweetheart, you and Patty can have some girl time, and I will be back before you know it."

"I love spending time with Patty. Right, Pats? But I want my man back as soon as possible."

Patty put her arm around Gemma and said with a wink, "We are going to have the best time! How many single men do you know?"

"Bill Smith, poor man, is alone this weekend, too. I bet he'd keep us company while you're gone," Gemma said hopefully.

Caleb replied, "I think that he went to Rhode Island to meet with the Association. When he gets back and I get back, we can all go down to the beach for a picnic, if you understand my meaning."

"I certainly do", Gemma replied with a mischievous little smile.

Gemma said to Patty, "I still have my little black book, but you can't fool me. I know you've had the hots for Harry for a long time."

"Yes, I have, and he's been holding out on me. How many naked selfies does a girl have to send before a man gets the message?"

Cal looked over at the two women and laughed. "With Harry, both of you could walk over and sit on his face, and if he was in one his thinking moods, he might not get the message. But if he is ready, watch out! You would be in for one hell of a ride, I bet."

"Well, then, Cal, give him this. Maybe this will get me some attention." She handed her brother a smallish package wrapped in festive paper, tied with a ribbon.

"What is it?" Cal asked.

"Something for Harry and none of your business," Patty said with a bashful smile and red cheeks.

"Patricia Smith, you're blushing!", said Gemma. "I've never seen you so much as blink an eye when you walked around your parents' house stark naked in front of your own father! I know what's in that package."

"You keep it to yourself!" Patty said with a wink at Gemma as she plopped down in a big, comfy chair with Barney the beagle.

"What the hell is it?" asked Caleb again.

"Never you mind. Just come back fast," Gemma said, now putting her arms around her husband and resting her head on his broad chest.

"Soon as I can, hon." Cal looked at his watch. "Man, I had better get going. The last ferry is in thirty minutes, and I need to see Harry tonight."

He kissed his wife deeply and then kissed his sister and Barney on the forehead. With that, he picked up Missy, all eleven pounds, and she licked his face. Missy did not want him to go, either. Last, he picked up little Jacob, just a little bigger at twelve pounds, and Jake clung to Cal like glue, his little tail going a mile a minute.

CHAPTER BOSTON

Caleb parked his car in the line waiting for the ferry to the mainland. He always used this time to think and meditate. Ferry time seemed to stretch out and take longer than normal time. Ferry time was filled with scents and sounds and sights that Cal did not have in his everyday life.

He relished this time and would sometimes, when he was younger, take the three-hour ride to Massachusetts for no other reason than to sit and think and be alone. Later, he would take Gemma on these rides, saying nothing to her for most of the trip, only holding her hand while she nestled up to him. The bonding they did on these sexless make-out sessions served them well to this day.

He watched gulls dip and swoop, dropping conch shells on the parking-lot pavement to crack them open. Some gulls flew overhead with spider crabs in their beaks, and others seemed to be content to ride the waves of wind.

Ah, there she is, thought Caleb as he saw the biggest of the ferries come into the slip. The men who worked the deck hauled the chains and ropes used to fast the vessel to the ramp. These men moved in a rapid symphony of well-rehearsed motion.

He watched all the cars and trucks that were heading onto the island disembark. There seemed to be a lot of them today, especially for a weekday.

One car caught his eye. It was black, one of those European supercars seen only on TV and the mainland and never on the island. Cal thought that it was fortunate that it was neither high nor low tide. A car that low to the ground would not get off the ferry unless the ramp and the ferry were perfectly lined up.

Cal made a mental note about the high-end automobile, but he had too much on his mind to think about it now.

The ferry ride was a long one, and Cal passed the time by reviewing his notes and sleeping. When he arrived in Boston Harbor, he was both up on all the details of the case and refreshed.

As he pulled up to Harry's lab, a large Colonial-era building with a sign carved in American walnut reading "THE HELLHOLE" affixed above the front entrance, he saw Doc Alchurch's new car, painted in a deep crimson, sitting in one of the reserved spaces. Cal knew this was the doc's car because he had asked Cal about what sort of car to buy before he made the purchase. It was a low-slung sports car of the air-cooled, rear-engine variety with a license plate that read "BLOODNGUTS."

The parking lot was not paved over. Instead it was all grass, the odd thing being that none of the grass was dead or worn away where it ought to have been, given the amount of traffic that it must endure. Cal wondered how Harry had managed such a feat.

Though the lab sat just on the outskirts of the city and still very much in an urban area, Harry had been able to buy all the land for many blocks in every direction and had knocked down all the buildings that did not suit his purposes. The now mostly empty lots were being transformed into native forest. There was a North American primeval forest starting to grow in Boston and it affected Caleb in an unexpected way. He felt oddly at home here as if he could remember being here, in the forest before, though that was impossible he told himself. The buildings left standing were those of historical significance, carefully turned into researchers' residences and other useful buildings.

This was how Harry intended it. When Caleb had asked him why he had bought all that land just to level it, Harry responded that he needed a connection to the Earth and nature to properly do his work.

There was even a café that was so good it had begun to attract the patronage of locals from surrounding areas.

Harry's had become the most prestigious forensic laboratory in the country. Some time ago, he had ended his role as the primary researcher, as the business had grown too large for him to do all the work himself.

These days Harry had a more managerial position, but this case was different. Caleb had specifically asked that Harry work on this case himself. The happy addition of Edgerton Alchurch to the research team gave Caleb further confidence that answers would be found.

Once inside the lab, Caleb walked through several sets of doors and was checked at each by facial, retinal, and voice recognition software he himself had designed. Now, deeper into the offices, he could see that the old Colonial building was backed by a huge structure that had a long, wide central hallway, on either side of which stood the labs and equipment. The tools and machines found here were found nowhere else in the world, because most of it had also been designed by Caleb.

Harry walked over to Cal and gave him a bear hug. "Hello, old man. So glad to see you. You've got to see what we have discovered."

"Caleb, my boy." Dr. Alchurch grinned.

"Hello, Doctor. Good to see you again. Miss the island?"

"I get back from time to time. How's the new doctor working out?"

"He's OK, but no one knows the residents the way you do."

"Ah, yes, he'll get there. He will. Look at this." Alchurch opened a drawer in his desk and pulled out some photographs and handed them to Cal.

"You'd never know, would you, my boy?"

Cal carefully looked over the photos of a pretty woman who looked to be in her late teens or early twenties.

"They look better than even I imagined they would, doc. I guess that software patch I sent over did the trick."

"It sure did," said Harry from behind Caleb.

What Cal held in his hands were not photographs, though not even the most skilled expert in the world could have deduced that, even on very close examination. What Caleb was looking at were computer-generated images of the girl whose bones lay in an examining room some distance down the main hallway.

Dr. Alchurch led Cal to that very room, passing a dozen others, all with doctors and technicians working on other cases.

When the trio reached the examining room in which lay the remains of the girl killed in the school, Caleb was shocked to find that he could be surprised. There before him was what looked like a body under a sheet. The part that shocked Cal was that the body appeared to be floating above the exam table. "Why does the body—or the bones—look like they're floating under the sheet?"

"That's because the bones are floating under the sheet," Harry said.

"Why are the bones floating, Doc?", Cal said in a dead-pan voice.

"We don't yet know, Cal," said Harry. "We can push her down to the table, and she'll stay there for a while, but she always goes back to that same distance above the table: 16.9164 centimeters. I'll leave it to you to see the significance of that measurement."

"I see the significance, Harry. I hate this mystical shit."

Dr. Alchurch excitedly added, "Caleb, you are the smartest man I know. When will you learn to not be afraid of that fact?"

"Never."

"Well, the floating bones are not the craziest thing about this."

"OK, what's the craziest thing about this?"

"Well, we found a long blond hair dried in the blood on the back of one of her femurs. It's old. Very, very old. Radiocarbon dating puts it at about seventy-five thousand years, the same age as the tooth we found."

"And yet it looks like a modern, ordinary blond hair? Bullshit," said Caleb dryly.

"Bullshit, you say?" replied the doctor. "Bullshit it may be, but the tests do not bullshit us. And that's not all. To get the full effect of the floating bones you've got to see her without the sheet." Alchurch brushed past Cal and pulled the sheet off the bones.

Caleb saw the girl floating above the table. He waved his hand under her. There was nothing there. Cal, even though he knew ahead of time that the bones were floating, was still amazed.

Harry said, "Man, oh, man. There's even more."

Dr. Alchurch held up the sheet for Caleb to see a perfect image of the girl's face and body on the sheet—not an image of her skull and skeleton, an image of her face and body.

"There's still more, my boy," said Alchurch, unable to contain himself. With that, Harry waved his hand across a pad on the wall next to the door. The windows went dark, and the lights in the room went out.

"Let your eyes adjust, Cal." Caleb waited a few seconds, and then he could see small glowing lines wherever the blade of the knife had made contact with the bones.

Harry tried to continue, but Cal interrupted him. "I know about this, Harry."

"You know about what?"

"About glowing marks on the bones. When I was doing a little research in Damascus, I went to the Mariamite Cathedral of Damascus to read some very old texts. Those texts made mention of executions and "marks made of the blade that shone in the night." I bet that if you look a little more into this, you will find that the knife's origin is more likely Syria than Jerusalem."

CHAPTER NEXT

Gemma had gone to Boston to meet with her spiritual adviser, Sister Maria Theresa, a Cistercian nun, but sister had had to leave on an emergency, so Gemma occupied herself with Museums, restaurants and visiting her old sorority at Wellesley. Gemma walked the streets of Boston alone in the late evening, deep in prayer. She was at a loss as to how she could help her husband. She was quite sure that the answer was in prayer. Gemma was certain of that.

She stood on the steps of the Cathedral of the Holy Cross and hesitated. The steps were wet with a rain that had stopped some minutes before. Her broad-brimmed rain hat still had drops clinging to it, refusing to drip off, she thought, as if being cheered from below to not do it. *Don't jump!* The thought made her smile at the whimsy of it. Gemma needed that little boost from inside herself, because she had felt so serious lately.

There was much to feel serious about. There had been the murder of the girl in the school, yet unsolved, though Gemma knew who was behind it, really. There was Caleb, so lonely inside himself. He had, of course, gotten involved in the murder case, but this new twist with his depression was something else she would have to deal with. He had become so very turned in on himself.

For a while she had known that there was much more than just the murder on his mind. That had upset him. It upset everyone, but the poor girl's death had not turned him somber. In fact, he felt energized, because he had something to focus his vast mental powers on. He had a puzzle to solve and justice to bring to the victim. No, the murder had not turned him so depressed.

She had puzzled over it herself for some time, and then in a dream it was all answered. One night, while asleep next to Caleb, she had been awakened by a loud bang from somewhere in the house. She sat bolt upright and looked over at Cal, who was still sleeping next to her. She looked at the foot of the bed, and the dogs were sleeping. The dogs seemed be able to tell if a rabbit was even thinking of hopping onto their turf and would respond with barking and howling at the slightest disturbance.

This was very odd, she thought. She would have been scared if Caleb's muscular form and Missy's mouth full of teeth had not been there to protect her. Still, they had not stirred, even a little, and that did frighten her. As she looked over at Caleb and watched his chest move up and down from his breathing, she heard a voice come from the doorway. "Hello, Gemma."

She instinctively clutched her covers to her chest, even though she was fully clothed. A figure, the Dark Angel, stood in the doorway and spoke again. "Hello, Gemma. I see you've got your man. What are you going to do with him? Love him? Help him? Save him? Maybe, but maybe not. I'm going to kill him eventually."

"He's my husband now. I will take care of him; I will love him; I will save him." Gemma sat there, not knowing what else to do or say.

The Dark Angel went on, "You can't be that surprised to see me. I've been in your husband's head for some time."

With that, it all started to make sense to her. Gemma was dreaming. She was dreaming but aware, and the Dark Angel was in her dream.

"Gemma, you've already lost. Caleb is as good as dead."

"You are able to torment Caleb because I let my prayer life go at the wrong time. I will not make that mistake again. Now get out of my house and go to hell, where you belong." With that, she turned over and went back to sleep.

Gemma continued up the steps of the cathedral and opened the door, which creaked on its hinges. The smell of 140 years of incense and candle wax washed over her, and she felt as at home here as in her own church. The vast vaulted ceilings soared above her, bringing to Gemma the feeling that Heaven was just there—just out of her grasp, but close—almost close enough for her to touch. The rows of columns marched beside her, holding up the sky of Heaven and giving her the sense that an army of the Angelic Host was at either side, ready to protect her and all creation if need be.

Gemma walked over to a pew, listening to the click of her high heels echo against the marble walls, sounds chasing sounds, finally hiding in the silent cracks and crevices of the old church where also hid a thousand memories, a thousand ghosts, a thousand souls saved from a forever in hell.

She genuflected at the entrance to the pew in the direction of the Blessed Sacrament, and with a gesture made unconscious by years of repetition, she reached out with her right foot, opened the kneeler, and went to her knees, holding a crystal rosary in front of her. Silently the Hail Marys poured from her mouth and flowed across the pews in front of her. Ten Hail Marys, one Glory Be, one Our Father, five times, ten times, twenty times over. As she continued to pray, Gemma began to rock back and forth, and her hands gripped the rosary beads tighter and tighter until, by the time she got to the fiftieth decade, her fingers were bleeding from the tips. Now there were no whimsical thoughts about raindrops, and, in the heavy quietude of the cathedral, the ever-so-faint sound of drops of blood hitting the marble floor could be heard.

CHAPTER NEXT

Father Christoph, a strongly built tough guy with graying temples and a hard-bitten face, whose congregation included those who lived in cardboard shelters down dark alleyways, worked street corners in the sex trade, and panhandled for drug money, woke five minutes before his 3:00 a.m. alarm sounded. He threw off his covers, swung his legs out of bed, and was on his feet, thinking about how he would battle the Evil One today—but not before he lit up the last of yesterday's cigar. He watched the smoke rise and decided he would offer a prayer to rise with the cigar smoke for the strength to face the day.

He took a bottle of bourbon from his nightstand drawer, poured two fingers into a glass, made the sign of the Cross over the glass, and downed the liquor. The bishop officially frowned on smoking and strong drink but pretended to not notice in the case of Christoph, because he was willing—eager, even—to take on the jobs that no one else would touch.

He put out the remnants of his cigar in an ashtray made from an old shell casing and stood up on the creaky wooden floor. He showered and dressed and was starting down the stairs when he felt that he might not be alone. He shrugged it off but still made a little mental note about the feeling. He went out the front door of the rectory and over to the cathedral, ready to say the Morning Office in front of the Blessed Sacrament.

There was that feeling again—that feeling of not being alone. Father Christoph had learned long ago to pay attention to feelings or proddings that happened more than once. Still, he did not know what to make of the feeling, so he went to his usual pew, knelt, and began his prayers. About ten minutes had gone by when he heard a rusty-sounding squeak come from behind and to the left of him. This alarmed him, and he stood and turned to see one of the hanging light fixtures swinging gently over a pew in the back of the cathedral. Christoph walked cautiously over to the pew below the light and saw a young woman on the floor, unconscious.

Father Christoph knelt beside her, put his hand on hers to rouse her, and noticed that her hand was covered in blood. She was holding rosary beads. He leaned closer to get a look at her face and realized that he knew this woman. "Gemma," he said in a gruff voice.

Gemma turned her head toward the voice and tried to focus her bleary eyes on the figure above her. She was unable to see clearly. She would have screamed, but for the fact that she could make out the white collar on the black shirt. In any case, screaming would have been impossible. Gemma found that she could not even speak at that moment.

"Gemma, Gemma Dufaigh," the figure continued. "Please, child, please wake up." Father Christoph helped her up onto the pew.

Every muscle in her body was sore, and she had a splitting headache.

Chris, getting a better look at Gemma's face and hands, gasped. He saw that she was clutching the rosary so tightly that she had broken her own skin; that was where the blood had come from. Her left hand had a cross cut into the skin on the top of it so that when viewed from Gemma's point of view, it was upside down. Her mouth was covered in dried blood, and her eyes looked black and blue and swollen, as if she had been on the wrong end of some tremendous fistfight.

The priest, who was the rector of the cathedral, asked, "Gemma, what has happened here?"

Gemma whispered through her painfully sore throat, "Father Christoph, is that you? Where am I? What time is it?"

"You are in the cathedral, and it's a little after three in the morning. What happened here?"

As he said those words, he reached for his phone and started to dial 911. "Gemma, I'm calling an ambulance. You look like you need real medical treatment."

She said, "Please, Father, no. Please don't call an ambulance. I don't need one. Please just take me somewhere so I can rest."

"That's not a good idea, but OK, for now." The priest helped Gemma up to her feet. Gemma looked up, her vision still blurry, and screamed hoarsely, bringing up blood that came out of her mouth and nose and landed on the floor.

Father Christoph asked, "What? What? What do you see?"

She could not answer. Her eyes were locked on the pendant lights, like the one whose swinging had alerted Father Chris to her presence. She tried to scream again and passed out in the priest's arms. What she had seen was the image of Caleb, hanging by his neck from a cord right where the lights ought to be.

Father Christoph picked her up and carried her to the front door of the rectory. When the pair reached the priest's residence, Christoph found an upside-down cross carved in the front door. His eyes got big, and his head pounded with a deep pain.

He said to himself, because Gemma was unconscious, "There is a powerful evil here. I've seen this before, and it is not pretty.

Gemma, you have tangled with something that probably should have killed you. Inside now, some tea for you and bourbon for me. Yes, there is nothing that whiskey and prayer cannot make at least a little better."

He had seen this before in Jerusalem when he was a young priest, sixty years ago. A group of Satanists had committed a series of grisly murders and had left this symbol behind at each one. Their leader was thought to be a young woman, though she was never caught.

There's no time for this now, he thought. *I must get this girl inside.*

Once inside, the priest laid Gemma on the sofa and went to the kitchen to put water on to boil and pour himself a drink.

Drink in one hand, kettle on the stove, Father Christoph picked up his phone and called his old friend and classmate Father John Smith, a not-too-distant relative of Caleb's but one who had kept his existence hidden from Caleb and his siblings. Arthur Smith knew him well, tough. They were second cousins and close friends. Given the kind of work that Caleb did, both men thought it best to keep Father John's identity a secret until such time that it became necessary to reveal himself.

"John, Christoph here. They're back, and they have a young woman in their sights for some reason."

"I know, Christoph—not about the woman, but that they were back."

"They left their 'calling card' with you, too, then?"

"Yes. They're trying to scare us. Good luck with that."

"Do you still have your weapon, the one from our army days?"

"Oh yes. I keep her cleaned and at the ready."

"Good. Me, too. I feel we may need them. Ah, I'm getting a call from your young relative. I'd better take it."

"Certainly, Christoph. Call me when you're ready."

"Absolutely. Out." Christoph switched calls. "Caleb, my boy! Where are you?"

"Hello, Chris. I'm in Cambridge. I was just here last week to look at something for a case in Harry's lab, sorry I didn't stop by then. I came back today to pick up my wife. Gemma said that she was going to the cathedral to meet with Sister Maria Therese. Have you seen her?"

"As matter of fact, I have. She's asleep on my sofa. Sister is on some business in France. That does explain a lot."

"Explains what, Father?"

"Well, I found your wife in a terrible state in the cathedral not twenty minutes ago. I don't know what happened, but it was not good."

"Damn it. Is she ok?"

"Yes, son. She's banged up pretty good, but nothing that won't heal. I'd love to know how this happened to her."

"I think I know, Christoph. I will be there in twenty-five minutes."

With that, Gemma roused herself from her slumber and walked unsteadily into the kitchen to find a cup of tea, some biscuits, and her husband on the phone.

CHAPTER NEXT

Caleb pulled up to the priest's residence in a new American muscle car that he had purchased several days prior and had picked up that day.

As he walked toward the front door of the rectory, he could feel someone with him. The presence was not friendly, and Caleb mentally moved into defensive mode, preparing for what could be a fight, but with whom, he did not know.

He saw the cross, upside down, carved in the wood of the door, and like Father Christoph, he remembered seeing the same thing in both Russia and Israel. From what Christoph had told him on the phone—and by the looks of the door of the rectory—his wife must have gotten herself tangled up with some very nasty things indeed.

Just as he was about to knock on the door, he heard from somewhere far off the howl of a wolf or a dog. If it was a dog, it was like no dog he had ever heard before. Suddenly he felt a searing pain in his right arm. He looked down to see his arm bleeding from puncture wounds. He felt and heard the bones in his forearm cracking and the flesh being ripped away. He let out a deep yell.

As he looked down again, he saw his arm completely whole. The wounds were gone. He stood there for a few seconds before knocking on the door.

Father Christoph answered. "Come in, Caleb, come in. Were you just yelling?"

"Father, did you hear anything just now, I mean besides my yelling?"

"No. What are you talking about?"

"Nothing. Nothing. Just stubbed my toe." Caleb said, stepping into the house.

Christoph raised his eyebrows at Cal, indicating his disbelief at what Caleb had told him, but said no more about it.

Gemma, hearing her husband's voice, came running out of the kitchen and threw her arms around his neck.

Cal, breaking their embrace, looked at his wife.

"Gemma, love, can you tell me what happened? You look like you've been in a fight!"

"I suppose if you put it that way, she was in a fight—a larger fight than she knows," said the priest.

"Caleb, honey, I was praying for you, for us, in the cathedral, and I saw you in a vision, falling into darkness, drowning, being attacked by wolves. The wolves had no eyes."

"Sweetheart, it was just a dream."

"No, no, it was not a dream. I was awake when I saw the wolves. You were being attacked, and you were drowning in darkness. It was as if the darkness was alive. It was swallowing you!"

"It's OK, baby. I'm here," Caleb said as he held his wife close and kissed her on the top of her head. He did not tell her what had happened to him at the front door of the rectory with the sound of wolves and the bites on his arm.

Father Christoph put his hand on Caleb's shoulder and said, "Son, it's not safe in this city for you or your wife. You can take care of yourself, but Gemma needs to be out of Boston."

Outside, a young blond girl stood at a window looking at the trio who had now moved into the parlor to talk. As she watched, a low growl came from her throat. With that, she vanished as Cal approached the window to open it.

He turned to Gemma and said, "We can't stay here. You can't stay here. Whatever is chasing me is now chasing you, maybe to distract me. Maybe it's to try to get to me through you. I don't know, and I don't want to find out."

CHAPTER NEXT

He was a man who could not control his thoughts. From the time of his childhood, voices had spoken to him, telling him to do unspeakable things.

So far he had been able to restrain himself, but tonight something was very different. He was dreaming. That much he was sure of. So many dreams. He was tiring of them. Why wouldn't they leave him alone?

"OK," he said, "if I do this thing for you, will you all please leave me alone?"

"We told you so. Don't you believe us?"

"Not anymore. You've made that promise before. I am so tired. Please just let me sleep."

"Sleep will come soon enough. Take this, and do as we ask."

The man was handed a knife. The knife was very heavy in his hands, and the blade had markings on it that the man could not read.

It had a plain wood handle, but the oddest thing about it was that it seemed to be drawn toward the girl. It was as if, had the man let go of the knife, it would have plunged itself into the girl's flesh of its own accord.

"Do it now," the voices commanded.

The man took a step toward the girl who had been in front of him the whole time. Tears ran down her face, and he could see her shake with fear as he moved closer. He raised the knife and brought it down with a guttural yell on her right shoulder. The blade cut through her tissues with such ease that the man, startled, stepped back, eyeing the bloody knife.

The cut was so quick and so clean that the girl stood looking at the man for several moments, tears still pouring over her cheeks, before she crumpled into a pile of fleshy bones and blood on the floor.

"Put this around her neck and tie her to the hook on the ceiling."

The man did as he was told. He was amazed at how easy it was for him to lift the girl. Then he was floating toward the ceiling, cord in hand, and he remembered that this was all just a dream, a very bad dream.

The girl made a few gurgling sounds as he looped the cord around the hook. When he was back on the floor, they said to him, "Pull her up and finish the job."

He found himself in the air again, floating just inches from the girl's face. The man threw his head back, screaming, and plunged the knife into the girl with impossible ferocity and speed. Flesh exploded from the girl's body like bloody fireworks. The man then dove face first at the girl and began to ravenously gnaw at her bones. He floated back, blood staining his face and sinew hanging from his mouth.

He realized what he had just done and began to scream. "God forgive me, please."

"God forgive you? How do you think you can be forgiven?" they asked. "We will see you again when we need you."

"No! You said that this was the last time. You said that you would leave me alone."

"Yes, we did. Now we are saying that we will see you again when we need you."

They who had been speaking receded further and further into the darkness, leaving the man alone. He found himself hanging by a lamp cord around his neck, his eyes staring into the empty eye sockets of the girl. He could just make out, in the faint light, a Saint Theresa medal hanging around the girl's bony neck.

The man choked and spit. His hands grasped at his own neck. The girl stared back at him, and he sobbed through his choking, writhing in remorse.

In the next moment, he sat up in bed, knife in hand. Blood drenched his bed. The man looked in the mirror facing the bed and saw a Saint Theresa medal hanging from his own bruised neck.

Just then, he heard a knock on his door. The man went cold. The blood, the knife! He could not hide them. He closed his eyes, and the knock came again. He opened his eyes, and the knife, the blood, and the medal were gone. The knock came a third time, this time with more insistence.

He got up, stumbled to the door, and opened it. Before him stood Caleb Michael Smith.

"Sir, we have to speak. May I come in?"

CHAPTER ORA—THE MYSTERIOUS WOMAN

She was delicious. She was cold. She was calculating. The woman was devious. She was delicious. She had entered the house uninvited and lay there on Caleb and Gemma's bed, nude and tan, green eyes glowing unnaturally, head propped up on Gemma's pillow. She had skin the color of caramelized sugar.

Her hair, beach-bum blond, framed a face that could have been on a box of Ivory Snow. Her legs were long and lean, curvaceous and smooth in a way that made a man's chest hurt. As Caleb's brother had put it so well, "She had legs that made you both grateful and sorry to be a man." So many men wanted her. So many. She had been with quite a few of them.

Afterward, most of these unfortunates would have given nearly anything to have *not* been with her. She had a way. Seductive was not the right word for it. Ordinarily beautiful women could be seductive. This woman was a black hole of salacious desire. She was the electric bug killer of men.

Men, drawn to her against their better judgment, their convictions, the pleading of friends, even their marital vows, got caught on the hot grid of her charged web and exploded as a jolt of hell shot through them, killing their souls from the inside out.

CHAPTER NEXT

In the gloom of the Autumn evening, Caleb walked across his front yard over to the path that led to the front door. He and Gemma had just arrived back from Harry's lab and the cathedral in Boston, and he just wanted to sit with his dogs in the house and chill. Gemma, still refusing medical treatment, was out buying groceries for that night's dinner.

The driveway, the staircase up to the house, and the path that led between them had been built from stones recovered after Boston's Big Dig tore up 250-year-old streets. He had built them all, laying stone after stone in local beach sand, pounding the smaller ones home with a rubber mallet.

He walked the path to his house. It was bordered on both sides by a tulip garden and lit with soft blue footlights. The whole effect was to welcome him home.

He was indeed welcomed home as Jacob, all-around good guy, heard him pull up. He ran out the doggy-door to greet his papa. Jacob bounded down the stairs and all but ran into Caleb, he was so excited. Caleb picked up Jacob, smooched him on his little face, and said, "How's my boy?"

Jacob was one of the reasons Caleb got up in the morning and one of the reasons he came home at night. Jacob's tail was wagging hummingbird fast, which usually meant that he was happy, but this was different. This was the nervous Jacob. Cal tucked him under an arm, saying, "Scoop up the pup!" to Jake, knowing that it was nonsense, but not caring.

Caleb walked the remainder of the path, ascended the stone stairs, whose steps were also lit by the same blue light, and put his hand on the latch. The door was unlocked, which was unusual these days, given the ghastly nature of what was going on. Caleb slowly pushed open the door. The hinges squeaked, and the sound echoed in the little house, making it sound much bigger than its 950 square feet.

Missy lay on the sofa, looking, for the entire world, afraid and timid. This was not the Missy Caleb knew. She would normally be barking and jumping all over him. He walked over, sat down next to her, and scratched her behind her ears, and she gazed up at him with that look. It was the look she used to give him when she would get into the garbage while he was out and she knew she had been bad.

Caleb said, "What's the matter, girl?"

She whimpered at him and licked his hand. That's when Caleb smelled it—the odor of sulfur and patchouli—an odor that he remembered from his nightmares from his adolescence, and sadly, more recently, that carried with it the feelings of hate, longing, lust, and repulsion. He knew where it came from without having to look and see. She was in the house.

Her underwear, sky-blue cotton bikinis, still warm from her body, were on the floor, and her bra was thrown on the chair next to the bed. Up close she smelled of salt air and sex and desire. She always had the faint smell of the beach and sex about her, and she knew it. She liked it. She used it to her advantage every day.

Her hair, not nut brown as Gemma's was, but blond, was spread on the pillow under her head, and her legs were spread slightly, just enough to give him a glimpse of what many men might literally kill to have. Her body was lean and athletic from years as a beach-volleyball player. She generally walked around in tight spandex shorts that accented her attributes in the most advantageous way, even though she would have looked at home in jackboots and an SS uniform—very Aryan master race.

She was physically spectacular and knew it. She was her own biggest fan. The only word to describe her was delicious. She was like an ice-cream cone in August, dripping down the sides, begging to be licked, though her heart was an icy conflagration.

Gemma loved Caleb. This woman did not care if Caleb lived or died, but Gemma had him, so to torture Gemma and Caleb, the woman wanted him. It's not that she did not find Caleb very attractive; she did. With his broad shoulders and tight stomach, his muscular arms and legs, his dark-brown hair and blue-green eyes, she had no problem lusting after him, and she wanted to satisfy her evil lust.

He had one gigantic flaw in her eyes, and that was that he was good. He was fucking good, and that turned the woman's stomach, because she saw it as a failing, a weakness. She was now out to spoil that goodness.

He was not the man she wanted him to be; her father had become that man. He could never be the evil, heartless man that she wanted. So now she wanted him dead—maybe not now, but at the right moment. However, if she could turn him and have him, she would have the best of both worlds. Too bad that he was content with his cameras, trains, computers, and dogs. Most infuriating to her was that he was content with, and loved, Gemma.

She thought he was weak. The one thing she did not know about Caleb, the one thing he did not know about himself, yet, was that when tested, he would show the most unshakable, almost scary, strength and tenacity.

Caleb went to the bedroom door, looked in, and saw her in his bed. He said, "What in blazes are you doing here?"

She ignored the question but replied, "Listen, how could you love that goody-goody? I mean, look at her." And taking a good hard look at his crotch, she continued in a leering voice, "Look at you."

Caleb slowly looked her up and down and said, "Gemma is *not* a goody-goody. She is good, period." Caleb continued, "What are you *doing* here, in our bed, naked? How did you get in the house?"

"If a man has to ask what I am doing naked in his bed..." She trailed off. "As for getting into your house, well, I have ways of getting to where I need or want to be. I can get into your dreams easily enough. Don't you get it? I can do what I want."

"I get it. I do. I know what you are capable of. There are no limits to your—"

She sat up. Her breasts, soft and round, bobbed ever so slightly; the skin on her chest just above her breasts was soft and tan, and it glowed with the light of a day in the sun.

"You need me! I can save you from a life of dull mediocrity!"

"But—"

She went on, "Maybe you really do need the saving. Your life is so boring. I bet Saint Gemma won't let you do anything. With me you could do everything, and I mean everything. Hell, I can tell you're thinking about it now. Don't you want it?"

She paused and smiled an innocent yet sexy smile, not real but crafted, not genuine but perfect.

"All of this"—she gestured to her own body— "and anything else you could think of could be yours for the taking."

"You've got to go. You've got to go now," Caleb said firmly in a steady voice.

"I've got to go? You don't want me to go," she said. "If you want me to go, why haven't you turned around? Why are you staring at my tits?"

Caleb wanted her to go, and he wanted her to stay in the worst way.

She went on, "You've had me in your dreams. Well, now you can have me for real."

"I would not call them dreams."

"Then I've been doing my job. Anyway, you can have Gemma, too. I don't give the slightest fuck. So, come over here and fuck me."

Caleb's breath had grown shallow. His stomach hurt. He did want to fuck her. He was holding on with all his strength, and in a move that nearly broke his neck, he turned away from her and stood there for a full minute. He then closed his eyes, turned around, walked a step closer to her, put his hand into his pocket, and took out a cheap, plastic rosary. He opened his eyes, took another step toward the woman in his bed, and held it out to her. As he held out his hand, rosary dangling from his fingers, he saw the faint outline of a face in the darkness outside his window, and his skin grew cold. The woman, who had looked so beautiful a moment ago, also seemed to take on a darkness that chilled him to the bone.

"Did you see someone?" she asked. The face grew more visible in the darkness outside the bedroom window. It was the face of a young girl, blond, with vacant eye sockets staring at him, empty and sick. She wore a smile, and a tiny drop of blood pooled at the corner of her mouth and started to drip down her chin. She not so much looked at him as leered in a taunting manner.

As Caleb stood there, staring back at the apparition in the window, the girl's face changed, growing as wrinkled and gnarled as tree bark. Her eye sockets went black, her jaw went slack. She raised an arm, pointed a bony finger at him, and faded from view. Caleb took a step back, dropping the rosary. He looked at the woman in his bed.

For an instant, her face took on the hag-like countenance of the apparition and then returned to normal. She sat up on the edge of the bed, still naked, and he noticed another drop of blood in the corner of her mouth. She took the middle finger of her left hand, wiped the blood from the corner of her mouth, put the finger on her tongue, and sucked the blood off, saying, "Mmm."

She stood up, grabbed the rosary from the bed and handed it back to Caleb. She got close enough for him to smell her hair, and her nipples rubbed on his shirt. Caleb stepped back, nearly tripping. She grabbed for the rosary, and his weight, falling backward, broke the thin string holding the beads together. Beads and Crucifix careened into the air, landing on the floor. She looked down at the broken rosary.

She laughed a little. "I hope your faith is stronger than *that*, Cal." She then placed two fingers inside herself and put her hand up to his face. It was almost too much for him to bear. Cal did not turn around. He took her wrist in his hand and shoved it from his face.

"You are pathetic," he said. "Little tramp, used to getting her way because of her body. Well, I am not one of your spineless little boys. You cannot lure me in that easily."

"Seems to me," she said back, "that you are easy enough to lure in. I'll have you, body, mind, and soul!"

"I will never, ever allow you to do that to me. God has my soul. It is not yours."

"It will be. Cal, you're just too damned stupid to see that my father and I have already won. We're leading you around like a puppy on a leash, chasing murdered bodies around the world. And for what? Nothing more than our own ends. You probably wouldn't be any good in bed, anyway. My father takes care of me. You are the pathetic one. So smart about books, so dumb about the people around you. So, little boy, when will you become a real man?"

Caleb looked over at his and Gemma's wedding photo on the nightstand. This gave him strength. "Get the hell out of my house, *now*." Caleb walked out of the room.

While he stood in the kitchen, he heard her getting dressed in the bedroom. Caleb thought of what desires had flashed through his consciousness. She had stood near him so close he could feel her warmth. He had been strong, he had resisted, and now those desires made him sick to his stomach. She was unbelievably beautiful, and he had almost let that beauty, the surface layer so easily scratched, under which lay a sewer of a woman, get to him.

The sound of her skirt being zipped up sent another wave of desire and nausea through him. She appeared at the door of the bedroom. Caleb turned his back on her while motioning for Jacob and Missy to come to him in the kitchen.

"Cal?"

Caleb ignored her.

"You can't be a good boy forever, Caleb Smith. I will have you."

From high above the little house watched Michael. He folded his wings behind him and was filled with a hard, stoney conviction that only the Angel who had defeated Lucifer could produce. Michael reached down from the ether and touched Caleb. Cal spun around and looked at the woman with Michael's steely gaze behind his eyes. The woman, being who she was, looked back into Caleb's eyes, saw that there was more than Cal standing before her, and was overcome by a fear the likes of which she had not felt since she was a little girl and her father had looked at her with just such a gaze.

Caleb spoke with the force of Michael's anger behind his words. "Get out *now*, or I will end you right where you stand."

She stepped backward, felt for the doorknob, opened it, and left the house as quickly as she could. When she got to her car, she found a note on the driver's-side front seat. She did not have to wonder who wrote the note. She knew. She bent down, picked up the folded paper, and read the words written in blood. She closed her eyes, got in the car, started the engine, and tore down the road.

CHAPTER NEXT

After Ora left, Caleb passed out on the bed just occupied by her. He woke up in his bedroom, the bedroom that he shared with Gemma who was visiting with Patty at his parent's house. He lay there on top of the wrinkled sheets that had covered Ora some hours before. He did not remember going to the bedroom or lying down. He was not even sure what hour it was. The window was dark. A small spear of light, thrown by the moon through the curtain, gave just enough illumination so that, when he held his hand in front of his face, he could just about see the outline of it. Caleb stared at his hand as if staring at it would bring back his memory of what had happened that day. He lifted his head and saw that his two doggy buddies were not there. He became frightened and called out their names.

"Jacob, Missy! Come! Where are you?" From the sofa in the other room, the two dogs ran into the bedroom. Missy, flew onto the bed and licked Caleb's face. Then Cal leaned over, picked up Jake, and lay back down with him on his chest. His heart felt a little lighter.

The sulfur-and-patchouli smell was still faint in room. It hung in the air like a funeral shroud. Caleb smelled it, just a little, and the day came rushing back to him. She had been here. She who invaded his dreams. He had been tested, and he had passed. He could not remember her face. Just like in his dreams, he could remember her voice, what she was wearing, and what she said, but he could not remember her face. He questioned whether anything had really happened. Was it a dream, too?

The cloud of depression descended over him once again. Cal put his head back on the pillow and fell asleep once again.

CHAPTER NEXT

He was just a little boy, a little five-year-old boy. He had celebrated his fifth birthday only the month before. The boy was named Aaron, but no one except his mother called him by that name. To everyone else he was Joey, so named because of the little front-facing baby-pouch that his mother had carried him around in for the first year of his life.

Aaron had woken up "in a mood," as his mother put it. He was cranky and angry that his father would not let him walk to school by himself. The school yard was only a few hundred yards from their house, and he was a big boy, after all. Nevertheless, his father took his hand and walked him to the schoolhouse and left his young son, with the frown on his face, in the care of the kindergarten teacher.

The father, being a kind and understanding man, hated seeing the look of disappointment in his son's eyes. So, he called the school and told them to let his boy walk home alone after school. The boy did not know that his father would be trailing behind him just out of sight, making sure that, even though the walk was very short, his little boy would be safe.

The boy stepped out into the beautiful Spring day. His lungs filled with the smells of freshly cut grass and warm earth. He had gotten the message from his teacher that he would be walking home alone. He was very excited at the news and felt like a big boy, just like the boys in the fourth grade, who were, it seemed to the boy, allowed to do anything. The boy's teacher had not told him that his dad was watching the whole time for the short walk home.

The boy started walking and was happily on his way home with the sun in his face. The father saw his son walking and smiling and singing to himself, and the father's heart nearly burst with joy and pride. The boy walked, and the father watched from a thicket on the side of the road. As the boy was passing his father, he stopped for a second and looked around, as if he knew he was being watched.

The sad fact was that the boy was being watched—and not just by his father. The father could not feel it; he was too old. The boy, well, the boy could feel it and felt the fear of being truly alone. The boy felt very scared but kept walking. He could see his dog standing in the driveway, his tail wagging. He could see his mother waving at him for being such a big, brave boy. The boy felt one last stab of fear and started to run toward his mother. His father saw his son take off running and was about to take off after the boy. Just at that moment, the father heard a twig snap behind him and turned for less than a second. Nothing. There was nothing there, so he turned back around.

His son was gone. The father bolted from his hiding place, dashing toward the house. When he got there, he saw no son, no dog, and no wife. The father's head began to spin. His son had been *right here* just a second ago. He felt like retching. He stumbled backward and fell, landing on his backside.

From the woods, next to his house, the father heard the word "Daddy!" just once. And then, silence.

CHAPTER NEXT

The game was on, the blood was pouring, and the evil that had taken the boy was ravenous for more. Soon the little island would be awash in the blood of the most innocent.

Joe Davis was a man, though he did not know it, who could trace his lineage back to James the Apostle, a fisherman.

He had had a long day so far. It had started at three in the morning, when he got up and went to the docks to his fishing vessel, the *Queen Bea*, named for his beloved wife, Beatrice.

The fishing had been good, and he had planned to return at four in the afternoon with his blues and haddock and cod on ice. The weather had been glorious, and the seas calm. A fishing captain could not have asked for more.

The strange and inexplicable events that were to take place during that day would change Joe Davis for the rest of his life.

The day's odd happenings began with a report over the radio telephone of a missing little boy, Aaron Taylor. The boy's father, William, was a great friend of Joe Davis's. Bill and Aaron had, just the week before, gone out with him fishing for fluke and stripers.

Aaron, despite being the youngest, had caught the biggest fish of the day: a forty-inch striped bass that had been cleaned, cooked over an open fire, and eaten in the evening twilight on the beach near where Joe docked his boat.

This was terrible news, for sure. Joe checked his lines and then went into the cabin to call his wife on his satellite phone. Gone were the days when his wife stayed home most days for fear of not being close to the radio if Joe radioed in. Satellite phones and sometimes cell phones had made communication with the mainland much easier.

Joe picked up the bulky handset and nearly dropped it on the deck of the cabin. He quickly punched the numbers for his wife's cell and said to himself as the call went through, "Pick up, pick up, pick up." His wife's sweet but troubled voice came over the phone and said to him, "You wouldn't be calling unless you'd heard."

"Yeah, I heard. What the hell is going on? Has Aaron been found?"

"No. He's still missing. The police are questioning Bill. He's a wreck. He doesn't know what happened—"

"What did happen?" interrupted Joe Davis.

"Well, nobody is really very sure. Bill said that Aaron was right in front of him, walking home, and then he was gone."

"Gone? From where?"

"From right in front of his house!"

"Goddamn it, goddamn it all to hell!" Joe yelled into the receiver. "How the hell could that have happened? This doesn't make sense." Joe heard a clicking noise on the line, and he knew that another call was coming through for his wife. "Who's that?"

"Holy crap, I have to go. It's Bill on the other line," his wife exclaimed.

"OK, just call me and let me know what the hell is going on." He pushed the end button on the phone.

Joe Davis placed the satellite phone next to the throttle control inside the cabin and just stared at the sea. He was pretty far out, Georges Bank, but not as far as the some of the sword boats. He couldn't make it back before evening, and he needed to haul in his lines.

Joe stepped out of the cabin onto the deck. He heard a despondent, frozen wail in the distance coming from the west. The blue sky had turned a pale, steely gray. The sea was as flat as glass, and there was not a breath of wind for as far as he could see. Finding the horizon was damned near impossible, and he got a touch of vertigo.

Joe stepped to the rail of the boat. What he saw made him lose his breath. The biggest wave he had ever seen, a green, watery claw, was rising in front of him, and before he could even scream, it was on him. The *Queen Bea* was capsized. He was sucked out of the upside-down boat and pulled deep into the maw of the sea.

Joe Davis struggled not to breathe in the water. The boat had turned over so fast, and he had been sucked under so quickly that he did not even have the time to realize that he was drowning.

Joe looked above him and saw the light of the gray sky filtering through the water getting dimmer and dimmer. With the last of the light, he was able to make out the satellite telephone sinking down past him along with the rest of his belongings. He tried to reach for the phone, struggling after it in vain as it sank to the lonely sea bottom. Joe knew it would have done him no good, anyway.

He tried to shout after it, mouthing, "Bea, Bea, Bea, please. I love you." This just brought water into his lungs, drowning him faster.

As he sank down below where the light could reach no more, he knew he was about to die. The cold of the water was numbing him, and he decided to not fight any longer and started to take the last breath of his life to end things right here, right now.

Joe Davis closed his eyes. Through his nose, he took in the icy water that would bring an end to a life that had been lived to his fullest capacity with the woman, the children, the friends, and the dogs who had meant more to him than anything else in the world.

At that very instant he saw a smiling face in front of him, a beautiful face, and an outstretched hand. He heard her say, clear as his ship's bell, "Joe, your time is not now. Take my hand."

Joe reached out for her hand, and as his fingertip touched hers, he found himself standing on the deck of his vessel, dry and safe, the satellite phone in his hand, his wife's voice calling to him through the speaker. "Joe! Joe! Joe, please tell me you're there."

Joe stood there, dazed. He looked at the satellite phone in bemusement. The sound of his wife's voice was the same as the voice he had heard when he was drowning. How had he not heard it then?

"Uh, Bea?" Joe stammered.

"Joseph Alexander Davis, I have been crying into this phone for a full five minutes. I could hear you choking. What's happening?"

"Ummm, I dunno, Bea," Joe said in a detached voice. "Bea, I love you." He ended the call, turned off the phone, and stared out at the sea.

"Fishing vessel *Queen Bea*, fishing vessel *Queen Bea*, United States Coast Guard Sector Boston, United States Coast Guard Sector Boston."

The radio broke the silence of the moment. He stepped into the wheelhouse, put the handset in its cradle, and picked up the mic of the radio. "Uhhh, Coast Guard Sector Boston, vessel *Queen Bea*."

"Joe, you OK? Bea called us here and said that you were acting funny."

"Yeah, Wyatt, I'm fine. Think I got a touch too much sun, or not enough sleep. Somethin'."

"OK, Joe. Glad that you're OK. Don't scare Bea like that, OK, buddy?"

"Sure, Wyatt, sure. I just need to pull my lines, and I'm outta here."

"Switch channel two-four, *Queen Bea*," Wyatt said.

"Switching two-four."

"Listen, Joe, Bea told me that you were acting strangely on the phone and that you hung up quickly and wouldn't talk to her. I've got to tell you that yours is not the only report of strange behavior on boats out on the Banks."

"How do you mean, Wyatt?"

"Well, we've had reports of men just jumping off their boats and trying to swim away in full gear. A couple have drowned. Three vessels have simply vanished off radar. Gone. We don't know what to make of any of it. We've got helicopters and cutters all over the place."

"Something weird happened to me, too, but I don't want to go into it now. I just want to get home before anything else happens."

"OK, Joe. You heard that the Taylor boy is missing? You heard about that?"

"I heard. Bea and I are pretty freaked out."

"Well, it's pretty freaky when it happens to people you know," said Wyatt. "OK, Joe, I will call Bea and tell her that you are fine and that you'll call her when you can."

"Thanks," Joe said.

"Switching channel one-six," Wyatt said.

"Channel one-six," Joe echoed.

"Fishing vessel *Queen Bea*, Coast Guard Boston Sector."

"Vessel *Queen Bea*, Boston Sector."

"As long as you are not in distress, Boston Sector out."

"Vessel *Queen Bea* is A-OK. Out."

Joe Davis did not know what to make of what had happened in the last hour. He was more confused and scared than he had let on. He sat down on one of the ice coolers and just stared out on the sea for another hour so that he could gather himself.

When he had sufficiently calmed himself, Joe Davis stood, went over to his lines, and began to haul them in. Hook after hook had fish, and not just fish. They were big, beautiful fish, silver and gray and blue and fat. He had never seen anything like it before: two hundred hooks, two hundred fish.

Joe methodically removed the fish from the hooks and iced them, all the while meditating on what had happened, making no sense of it at all but feeling a deep peace like he had never known before.

Fish hauled and iced, Joe cleaned up and went to the cabin, pointing the bow of the *Queen Bea* toward his home port, leaving the throttles at one-quarter. As his fish-laden vessel lumbered its way home, Joe picked up the satellite phone and dialed his home number.

Bea picked up on the other line and just sobbed and sobbed into her phone. Finally, after a minute of crying into the phone, she said, "Joe, I am so glad you're OK. What happened? Why did you sound so weird on the phone?"

Joe said, "Honey, you wouldn't believe it if I told you…" and Joe and Bea talked and talked in a way they had not done for a long time.

By the time he got back to North Island, it was midnight, and there was no one to help unload the catch. Instead of going home, waking the children, and then waking them again when he left to go back to the docks, Joe opened up a sleeping bag. As he was smoothing it out, he heard that same angelic voice from behind him call, "Joseph Alexander Davis."

CHAPTER NEXT

Aaron Taylor and Joe Davis, though Joe had not died, thank God, had been the last straw as far as Caleb was concerned.

During the evening twilight at the end of a beautiful day, very much like the one on which Aaron had disappeared, his body had been found in an open coffin in the local Presbyterian cemetery, dressed in his own Sunday best. Except for his face and head, every ounce of flesh had been removed from his body. The coffin sat next to a freshly dug grave and had been discovered by a man and his wife placing flowers on the man's long-dead mother's headstone.

Everything about it was as creepy and as horrible as it could be. Bill Taylor was not suspected in his son's disappearance; there had been people farther down the road that fateful day who told the police that they had seen little Aaron walking toward his house, his father trailing behind, watching his son. The mother and the dog were not missing. She had merely gone back into the house with the dog to answer a ringing phone. These witnesses had heard the boy cry out, "Daddy," had seen Bill Taylor running toward the last place his son had been, and had themselves run toward the scene to help, if possible.

CHAPTER NEXT

Caleb was in his livingroom, watching TV and eating the lunch prepared for him by Gemma. His phone lit up with a call and he saw the number: the BPD, Frank Coughlin to be exact.

"Cal Smith?" The familiar voice of Frank came over the phone. "Cal," the voice continued, "are you working on the Aaron Taylor killing?"

"Yes, Frank. There is not much to go on, but I have had the body sent to Boston to have Harry and Doc Edgerton do what they do."

"Damn, Smith, how could this have happened? Nobody is getting on or off that island without being searched. There aren't that many people to start with! The killer has to be on the island."

Since the first killing, Frank had asked that every single car, person, and bag be checked while boarding the ferry and disembarking. It was not that big a hassle, because there was only one ferry per day, and that vessel carried only fifteen cars at a time. Caleb had run the profiles of every single person on the island through his algorithm. The answer produced was too unbelievable to tell to anyone other than his wife.

"Listen, Frank, all I can tell you is that I am working on both murders and the Davis fishing boat incident, because I think that they are all related. That is all I am prepared to say for now."

Frank asked, "Why the Davis incident? What's that have to do with anything?"

"As I said, Frank, I believe that the boat thing is related to the murders. I spoke to Joe Davis and some of the things he said struck a chord. I won't say any more, because you wouldn't believe it, anyway."

Frank sighed on the phone, said "Fair enough", and hung up.

Cal stood up and walked into the kitchen. Jacob and Missy were sitting there, looking up at him expectantly. He sat down on the floor. Missy licked his face, and Jacob climbed in his lap. Even while fooling around with his dogs, Cal's mind was working on the problem at hand.

When Caleb asked, "Do you two want to eat?" the two dogs barked in excitement. They danced around his feet as he went under the sink, scooped out the food, and put it in one small bowl and one large bowl. Cal lifted himself onto the countertop and watched the dogs eat. The innocence and pure joy that they took in everything was beautiful to watch. He envied them. When they were with him, they were with him. When they were eating, they were eating. There was focus on, and gratitude for, what they had at the very moment.

Gemma was out front gardening so Cal, sitting on the countertop, fell into a meditative place. He was thinking on a conscious level, but more than that, his deeper mind was searching the world, other minds, even different realities for links and clues to what was going on.

Who was this Dark Angel that he so often felt was around him? Angels? They were the stuff of Bible stories and hallucinations. However, now he could not think about it. There would be time enough to dwell in the house of evil.

CHAPTER NEXT

Cal jumped down from the counter and went to his and Gemma's room to get dressed. He knew that there was only one thing to do: he had to find the source of the murders and the general evil that he saw gestating on his island before it became too strong to contain.

He wanted to call Harry. He picked up his phone and put it down again.

He stood in the room, stuck, wondering what to do. He picked up the phone, started scrolling again through the recent calls, and tapped the one for the Boston Police Department. The phone rang and rang, longer than usual. When his call was answered, he knew what had taken so long.

The voice of the chief of detectives said, "Caleb Smith, hello. I have been glad to have your help with these murders, but I do think that we have our man. You said so yourself."

"Chief Ó Briain, these killings do seem strongly linked to the man you have in custody. However—"

"Strongly linked? The suspect has the victim's blood under his fingernails, and some of the marks on her bones match his teeth."

"I understand, Chief, but the blood could have easily gotten under his nails when he was helping clean the classroom.

"Ahhhh, I don't want to hear this claptrap. The man we have killed the girl in the school and the boy, and that's that. We found skin cells from the suspect on the boy's clothes."

"That means nothing, Chief. The fact that the man you have was a janitor at the school and was friendly with the boy might explain the skin cells, too. There are just too many things that do not fit. If we stop looking and someone else dies, the blood will be on our hands, Chief."

"Balderdash, Smith."

"Look, Chief, a girl is killed, flesh not ripped but filleted from her bones so cleanly that it almost looks like the work of a surgeon. Further, it is not entirely clear how the girl came to be hanging from the ceiling. Your suspect is neither strong enough nor tall enough to have hung her there—even if he stood on a chair or desk—and we did not find anything on which he could have stood.

"Regarding Aaron, in the space of less than thirty seconds a boy, very nearly in the witness of his father, is snatched from a road in broad daylight—and in front of his own house, no less. Then he shows up dressed in his own set of clothes—not the ones he was wearing when he went missing, mind you—in a casket in the cemetery at his family's plot. This moron you have in custody is neither physically nor intellectually capable of pulling off something like that."

The chief said, "Smith, when you were first hired by the department, I was very skeptical. Now I know I was right to be. You're smart, Smith. Too smart by half, I'd say."

"Chief, I am not saying that this guy is not your man. What I am saying is that there are many things that point in another direction."

"Smith, I am not listening to any more of—"
Then silence…then a gurgling sound…then a man screaming.
Then silence again.

CHAPTER LAST

Caleb Michael Smith was sitting in a seat on a private jetliner owned by the Association. He felt his phone vibrating and saw a text from Gemma. "Please call me!"

He punched the numbers for his parents' house, which was where he had put Gemma and the pups while he was gone so that they would be safe.

"Honey, I have to go—you know that I do."

"I know, but I don't want you to! For how long this time?"

"Sweetheart, I don't know. The man who was in custody in Boston has been spotted by reliable witnesses in Jerusalem."

"But how? How did he do this terrible thing? How did he kill the chief and five armed officers?"

"That's what I am going to Israel to find out."

The captain's voice, sporting a thick Israeli accent, rang through the cabin. "Welcome to El Al flight thirty-three-thirty-three. We will be taking off in just a few moments, so we ask that you turn off your cell phones until we are at cruising altitude."

"Gemma, baby, I love you with all my heart. I have to go."

"OK, honey, I love you, too. Bye." Gemma hung up the phone and cried.

For his part, Cal leaned back in his seat, put his headphones in his ears, and started listening to his new favorite song, "Sympathy for the Devil."

Made in the USA
Middletown, DE
30 November 2016